Nathalia BUTTFACE

NIGEL SMITH has been a journalist, busker, TV comedy producer and script writer, winning an award for his BBC 4 radio comedy, *Vent*. More importantly, he has been – and still is – an embarrassing dad. Much like Nathalia Buttface, his three children are continually mortified by his ill-advised trousers, comedic hats, low-quality jokes, poorly chosen motor vehicles, unique sense of direction and unfortunate ukulele playing. Unlike his hero, Ivor Bumolé, he doesn't write Christmas cracker jokes for a living. Yet.

This is Nigel's fifth book about
Nathalia Buttface.

Nathalia BUTTFACE
and the Embarrassing CAMP Catastrophe

BY
Nigel Smith

Illustrated by Sarah Horne

HarperCollins *Children's Books*

First published in Great Britain by HarperCollins Children's Books in 2016
HarperCollins Children's Books is a division of HarperCollins*Publishers* Ltd,
HarperCollins*Publishers*, 1 London Bridge Street, London SE1 9GF

The HarperCollins Children's Books website address is
www.harpercollins.co.uk

1

Nathalia Buttface and the Embarrassing Camp Catastrophe
Text copyright © Nigel Smith, 2016
Illustrations copyright © Sarah Horne, 2016

Nigel Smith and Sarah Horne assert the moral right to be
identified as the author and illustrator of this work.

ISBN 978-0-00-816712-7

Printed and bound in England by
Clays Ltd, St Ives plc

To all the children who continue to share their embarrassing dad stories with me, especially their embarrassing names. To all the poor Milly Moo-Cows, the Katie Potatoes and the Tommy Blueberrys. To the Piglets, the Widgets, the Teabags.

Thank you for sharing, thank you for making me laugh, thank you for giving me stories I can totally nick.

CHAPTER ONE

. . . .

"And the winner is... Darius Bagley!"

THE Darius Bagley?

There was a stunned silence as the Head read out the shocking result to the whole school at assembly. It didn't just shock the school; it shocked her too.

The Head frowned and rubbed her glasses, peering at the envelope she had just opened. She *must* have read it wrong. But no – there it was in black and white.

Darius Bagley a *winner*? In an essay-writing competition?

"Essays? I didn't even know he could write," Miss Eyre whispered nastily to her equally nasty pal

Miss Austen, standing at the back of the hall. She made sure that she whispered it just loud enough for everyone to hear.

"He can't, much," said Nat to Penny Posnitch. "I wrote it for him. In fact, I spent so long writing HIS rubbish essay, I didn't have time to finish MY rubbish essay. The little cheaty chimp."

"You only wrote his essay because you owed him loads of favours – he's done every single one of your maths tests," giggled Penny. "You're just as big a cheat."

"That's different," muttered Nat, kicking at the floor.

"AND you told me you wrote it as a big joke," added Penny.

"It was a big joke. But, as usual, the joke's on me," said Nat sulkily. "I should be getting MY name read out on stage, not that tiny monster."

"He's won a prize," shouted the Head, continuing to read her letter, "an actual prize!"

"SO not fair," said Nat.

"Where is Darius Bagley anyway?" said the Head. "Come up here now and collect your prize so we can get this over with."

"He can't come up, Miss," shouted Nat. "He's sitting outside your office."

"Oh, surely he can't be in detention already," said the Head. "It's not even nine o'clock yet."

"He says it saves time, Miss," said Nat.

"I'll get him," said his 8H form teacher, Miss Hunny, chuckling.

A minute or so later, Darius trotted in, wearing his usual ripped blazer, torn jumper, grey-collared shirt, and egg-stained tie. He hopped on to the stage.

"HELLOOO, LOSERS!" he yelled, like a rock star saying hello to ten thousand fans.

Unlike a rock star in front of ten thousand fans, he got a lot of booing. A few scrunched-up crisp packets and a plastic pop-bottle whizzed towards him.

"What's my prize?" Darius asked the Head. "Is it sweets, a dog or an air rifle?"

"It's better than any of those," said the Head. "It's a book token."

"You keep it," said Darius, walking away without the token.

The school – including the teachers – burst out laughing.

The Head shouted crossly for silence. She grabbed Darius and thrust the token into his hands.

Darius turned away, skilfully making the token into a paper aeroplane as he went.

"Wait. I haven't finished with you yet," she said.

Darius stopped walking, plonked himself down on the edge of the stage and dangled his legs over it.

"This is a very important prize you've won," said the Head.

"Yes, but *I* won it," said Nat through gritted teeth.

"As you may know, children, this was an essay-writing competition organised by a charity that looks after our countryside. Their motto is: 'A tidy country is a happy country'."

Nat looked around at the litter-strewn school hall and sniggered.

The Head looked at it too, but just sniffed. She carried on: "Darius's prize-winning essay was called…" She frowned down at the letter. "Erm, his essay was called: 'Let's have less trees and rubbish flowers, more theme parks and oil wells'."

Nat chortled, remembering the fun she had writing it. All she'd done one night was scribble down the stuff Darius always said about the countryside. There was a naughty little part of her that had thought it might be funny to watch him getting told off yet again. But how on Earth did it win?

The Head continued, in a voice which suggested she'd rather be Head at a different school, "According to this letter, the judges said it was a hilarious but chilling satire on what would happen if a lunatic was in charge of the country."

Satire? *Satire?* Nat suddenly understood why Darius's essay had won.

"What's a satire?" Penny asked Nat.

"It means you're being ridiculous to be funny," said Nat.

"Like being sarcastic?" asked Penny.

"No," said Nat sarcastically. She frowned crossly. "But I wasn't being sarcastic – I just wrote down what Darius actually WANTS TO DO! He hates trees and flowers but he likes theme parks and oil wells. AND high-speed trains, quarries, and places where they test tanks."

She looked at Darius hogging all the attention and stamped her foot.

"None of this is fair," she shouted. "I want that book token. I like books – to read, and not just to make into paper aeroplanes."

"Can pupils please stop shouting out," demanded the Head. "I've got a coffee going cold in the staffroom and I'd like to get back to it."

By now everyone was a bit bored and restless so the Head raced through the next part as quickly as possible.

"Anyway, thanks to clever little Darius, his whole class, 8H, has won a super week at a special 'back to nature' campsite thing next month."

"Is HE coming?" shouted Julia Pryde, a girl from 8H, pointing to Darius and making a "yuk" face.

"Of course he is," said the Head, who was looking forward to a Bagley-free week. "After all, you wouldn't even be going if it wasn't for him. Now get to class – our exam results have been so bad recently I'm surprised we haven't been turned into a shopping centre."

Nat wondered how a campsite could be super. Super uncomfortable, maybe. Super damp, super bug-ridden, super grotty, yes.

But she was too busy getting swept up in the sea

of kids heading back to class to worry about it too much.

Anyway, a school trip, even if it was rubbish, meant no schoolwork so that was good news, woo!

"That is the worst news I've ever heard," yelled Nat that night.

She was in the kitchen with Dad, who was preparing his favourite meal, pork pie and chips.

"You don't mean that," said Dad, smiling. "Now, do you want any veg? I'm thinking baked beans."

"I'm thinking you *can't* come with us to the campsite for the week," said Nat. "I'm thinking it'll be rubbish anyway, but it'll be extra, super, luxury rubbish if you come too."

"Don't be daft. It's almost as if you think I'll embarrass you or something!"

"I do think that. I totally think that."

"You make me laugh when you get cross," said Dad, ruffling her hair. Which made Nat even crosser.

"When Dolores – Miss Hunny to you…" began Dad.

Nat groaned.

Her form teacher Miss Hunny and Dad were

old mates and that often led to mega-embarrassing times, like when she'd come home to find her teacher IN HER HOUSE, drinking red wine in her kitchen. Fortunately Dad was such a rotten cook that Miss Hunny didn't visit much. Nat started thinking about how terrible her life was…

"Pay attention," said Dad. "When Miss Hunny rang and told me Darius had won you that camping trip, I said that's great news because I need to get my Approved for Kids certificate."

Dad put on his patient face. "You know I've applied for a job – I told you, remember?"

"Oh yeah, Mum told me. She said she was fed up with going out to work all hours while you sat around in your pants writing Christmas-cracker jokes and eating pork pies all day."

"I don't think she put it quite like that," said Dad with a mouthful of pork pie.

"No, when Mum said it there were loads more rude words."

"Anyway," continued Dad, putting beans in the microwave, "I've got a job offer."

"A job? Like normal people? You? Doing what?"

"Teaching comedy skills to young criminals who

want to turn over a new leaf."

"What comedy skills? Your jokes were voted the worst Christmas-cracker jokes of all time by that website last year. You even got a prize – look."

On a shelf by the cookbooks stood a little plastic figure of a man holding his nose.

"You won a Stinker."

"A prize is a prize," said Dad proudly. "It makes me a prize-winning joke writer. At least that's what I tell everyone."

Nat stamped her foot. "But I still don't understand why you want to come on our school camping trip."

"Because the people who lock up the young criminals said that I need to have an Approved for Kids certificate to get the job."

"Find some other kids," said Nat. "There are loads of us – every town has them."

"No time," said Dad. "Plus the Head at your school knows me because I've done plenty of things there before. You know, until you banned me from doing them."

"Can you blame me, Dad?" said Nat, as the beans *pinged* in the microwave. Smoke poured out of the door. "Everything you do ends in total disaster.

You took my class to a boring cathedral and got us chucked out, and that was even *before* Darius went up on the roof and mooned the whole town. You put on a school quiz night that ended in a riot. You've sunk priceless sailing boats. You've got me arrested by real police. You've blown up houses—"

"Just one house," corrected Dad. "One tiny house."

"You've electrocuted the world's most precious ducks, you've ruined weddings, you've made me a laughing stock all over the Internet, AND you projected massive naked baby

pictures of me on a wall at the school disco."

"I was hoping you might have forgotten that one."

"How can I forget my bare baby bum, ten feet high on the gym wall at school? I can't forget it, and neither can the five hundred other people who saw it."

Dad made that noise which Nat recognised as his 'trying not to laugh because my daughter will get even crosser' noise. Which just made her crosser.

"AND you stuck me with the world's most embarrassing surname," she said.

"It's pronounced Bew-mow-lay."

"It's spelled B-U-M-O-L-E though, isn't it? I'm getting married at sixteen just to change it."

Before Dad could reply, Mum came bustling through the kitchen door, still in her coat and, as ever, texting on her mobile.

"Mum, Dad's trying to ruin my life again," said Nat, "and he's had loads of practice so he's got ever so good at it."

"I didn't know you were home for dinner tonight," said Dad, trying to hide his rubbish meal.

"Obviously," Mum said, kissing him fondly on

the cheek. She hugged Nat, still texting, and sniffed the beany smoke.

"Bin it. I'm taking you out for Chinese," she said. "Tell me all about it over crispy duck. I think you'll find it makes everything better. Even your daft dad."

CHAPTER TWO

• • • •

"I THINK WE ALL OWE DARIUS A BIG THANK-YOU," said soppy Miss Hunny in class the following week. "The camping trip sounds super brilliant."

Nat didn't care how super brilliant it sounded because it still looked like they were going WITH HER DAD, AAAGH.

She looked at Darius sitting next to her. He had bits of stringy snot dangling from each crusty nostril and she really hoped it wasn't just the one piece of string.

Miss Hunny burbled happily on. She was wearing a sun-yellow cardigan, and the long sleeves dangling over her hands spun round in excited little circles as she waved her arms around enthusiastically.

"We're going to make camp, and try rock climbing and pony-trekking, go exploring, practise map-reading and do other cool geography stuff."

"There isn't any cool geography stuff, Miss," said Nat, "because geography isn't cool. It's the least cool subject there is."

"Who said that?" said Miss Hunny.

"Mr Keane, the new geography teacher," giggled Nat. "It was when we asked him why he was crying at his desk last week."

"He made my homework all soggy," explained Penny, "and I'd spent hours drawing that unicorn."

"You really must stop drawing unicorns in every class, Penny," Miss Hunny scolded gently.

"Even in geography?" said Penny.

Miss Hunny looked at 8H with a mixture of affection and despair. Nat recognised the look: it was the look she often gave Dad.

"We're also trying to find super-rare fossils," said Miss Hunny, "and fossils are definitely cool."

Darius pulled a string from his nose and flicked it at the back of Julia Pryde's hair. "Nah," he said, "*dinosaurs* are cool. Fossils are rocks. And rocks suck."

"Language, Darius," said Miss Hunny.

"Do you want *this* language instead then?" said Darius, unleashing a stream of gibberish.

Except it wasn't gibberish. Parveen Patel shrieked and turned around in her chair. "Who taught you words like that?" she said angrily.

Darius then entertained the class with even more rude words in even more languages until he was told to sit outside the classroom. His excuse that he'd learned them as geography homework didn't work.

Miss Hunny kept Nat behind after class.

Uh-oh, thought Nat, *I'm in trouble*.

"Now, Nathalia, I don't think Darius wrote that essay on his own, did he?" said Miss Hunny, pulling up her sleeves. Nat shuffled her feet. "For a start, I could *read* it."

"I might have helped him a teeny-tiny bit, Miss," she admitted. She was pleased to FINALLY get the credit, but she was a bit worried she'd been caught cheating.

"I thought so," said Miss Hunny, "which makes you…"

Here we go, thought Nat, *that's me picking up litter all week*.

"…a kind and rather wonderful girl."

"Not fair, why do I have to pick up litter? I'm fed up of – oh." She paused. "Come again, Miss?"

"Like me, you see the good and the beautiful in Darius, where others only see naughtiness. Naughtiness, rudeness, untidiness, laziness, lateness, and a worrying fondness for farts, burps, bums, poos and – oh, do stop sniggering, Nathalia."

"Sorry, Miss. Don't mean to, Miss."

"Anyway, I've been asked to nominate a team leader for our camping trip. And I was wondering if you—"

"Would be the team leader?" interrupted Nat, eyes shining. "Oh, flipping heck, yes. That's brilliant, thanks very much. Winner, woo."

"No, I'm going to ask Darius to be team leader."

"What?" Nat felt like a spanner.

Miss Hunny smiled gently. "I think the responsibility will help him grow up."

I think you're barmy, thought Nat.

"I was going to ask if you wouldn't mind keeping an eye on him. Help look after him."

"Look after HIM?"

"Underneath that chimp-like exterior is a

vulnerable little boy, Nathalia."

"No there isn't. Underneath the chimp is a gorilla, trust me."

"Very funny. Just keep an eye on him. Would you do that for me?"

"Oh yeah. Well, of course. I mean, I don't want to be a stupid team leader anyway," fibbed Nat.

"You look a bit fed up," said Miss Hunny kindly. "Sorry, Nathalia, I didn't mean to get your hopes up. I was actually going to make you team leader but your father said I shouldn't put too much pressure on you because you're so delicate."

I'll show him how delicate I am when I get home, thought Nat.

Miss Hunny broke into a wide smile. "Oh cheer up. The REALLY exciting news is that we'll be *sharing* the campsite."

"Who with?" asked Nat.

"A lovely class from St Scrofula's School. They were the other local school to win the essay competition."

Miss Hunny said that as if it was a big deal.

"Big deal," said Nat.

*

"Actually, that IS a big deal," said Dad that night, as they drove home in his horrible, noisy, cluttered camper van, the Atomic Dustbin. "St Scrofula's is a top school."

"Don't care, Dad," said Nat, playing with the Dog in the back of the van. Her head was resting against a tent and some sleeping bags. They smelled of damp and mildew. *Urgh*, she thought, *camping. Yuk.*

"You *should* care. As it happens, your mum's often talked about sending you to that school."

A chill went down Nat's spine. It was hard enough making friends at her own school, which was a normal one, let alone trying again with a bunch of snooty kids. She had worked her way up from the bottom of the bottom group of popular kids to nearly the middle of the bottom, and she wasn't going to start at the bottom of the bottom again, thanks very much.

"It's dead posh," said Dad. "You'd like it. It looks a bit like a castle. It's got a full-sized football pitch, floodlit tennis courts, and an Olympic-sized swimming pool."

"So?" said Nat.

"All their kids go to top universities."

"You'd think they'd be too tired to learn much, after all that running and swimming," said Nat.

"They've even got their own school ponies," said Dad.

"We've got school rabbits," said Nat. "Well, we used to have school rabbits until the caretaker bought a new dog. Now we've got no rabbits, just a fat school dog."

Her own dog shook his whiskery head as if to apologise for the school mutt's doggy crimes.

"I bet the kids are stuck-up and horrible," said Nat, "which is rubbish cos even the girls in my class are a bit stuck-up and horrible – and they go to MY school and they haven't got anything to be stuck-up about."

"Give them a chance when you get to the campsite," said Dad. "You might make some nice new friends."

"I haven't even got nice OLD friends," muttered Nat. She settled down on the mouldy sleeping bag. "And please tell me you've listened to me and you're not coming. This camping trip's rubbish anyway – I found out it's all about geography."

"Sounds great. Rock climbing, canoes, caves, maps, fossils, all that stuff."

"Sounds rubbish. And you'll just find new and horrible ways to show me up."

"No I won't, I promise."

"And stupid Miss Hunny's made Darius Bagley team leader. AND I'm his babysitter."

"That was my idea," said Dad.

"Yeah, I know," sighed Nat. "Thanks."

"Anyway, responsibility is good for you."

"How would you know?" said Nat. "Mum's in charge of everything."

"Responsibility is good for SOME people," laughed Dad.

They drove in silence for a little while. Silence, that is, if you didn't count the racket from the dodgy exhaust. Nat's brain was racing ahead, writing a LIST OF DOOM. Worse still, at the back of her mind, a little nagging voice was telling her it was ALL HER FAULT. If she hadn't helped Darius with his stupid essay in the first place, they'd never be going camping.

The doom list seemed endless: rubbish campsite, week-long geography lessons, *Darius* in charge, Dad and his horrible little ukulele tagging along, snooty posh kids prancing about on their own ponies...

How bad was this week going to get? What else was going to go wrong?

Just then Dad hit a pothole and a frying pan slid off a shelf and clonked her on the head.

CHAPTER THREE

• • • •

"'LOWER TOTLEY IS A DELIGHTFUL TOWN, FULL of historic charm'," said Penny, sitting next to Darius and Nat on the back seat of the coach. "It says so on the town's web page."

"No it doesn't," said Darius, with an evil grin. "Not since ninja hacker Darius Bagley changed it."

"He's right," laughed Nat, who had helped Darius with the spelling. "It now says: 'Lower Snotley is a rubbish town full of historic zombies'."

"You make him worse, Nat, you really do," scolded Penny.

Nat stuck her tongue out at her.

Class 8H were on the coach to their super

geography camping experience thingy. They had been travelling for less than ten minutes and Nat was already a bit cross.

To be fair, she had been a bit cross the entire *week* leading up to the trip, so the torrential rain that had been hammering down like wet nails all morning wasn't likely to cheer her up.

"This campsite we're going to has a website as well," said Penny. "Don't tell me you wrote something rude on that."

"Nah," said Darius, "better than that. I put this picture on it."

He showed Penny a picture. She shrieked.

"And I can make *that* bit wiggle," cackled Darius, chewing a toffcc.

Penny peeped. "OK, now *that's* funny," she said.

"How about a singsong?" said Dad, standing up in the middle of the coach, holding his ukulele.

Nat threw Darius's toffees at him. "Go away, sit down, shush. No one wants to sing," she said.

"It is a bit early," said Miss Hunny from the front seat. "At least wait until we get there."

"Where we can hide in our tents," sniggered Miss Austen.

"With earplugs in," sniggered Miss Eyre.

Nat didn't know why Misses Austen and Eyre had volunteered to come, as they were the laziest teachers in the school and she couldn't imagine either of them rock climbing.

She grinned. She suddenly DID imagine them rock climbing. They were dangling in mid-air just as she pushed a massive boulder over the cliff…

PLINKY PLINK PLINK, went Dad on his stupid useless instrument.

"*Oh, we're off on a coach and it isn't very quick, but two of the class are already travel-sick…*" he sang.

"Join in on the chorus, kids," he said.

"Dad, we haven't got out of the one-way system yet and you're already showing me up," said Nat, jumping up and snatching his ukulele. "And you *promised* you wouldn't."

"I just want to make a good impression, for my certificate," whispered Dad, sitting down on the back seat. "Budge up."

He pointed to a man Nat didn't recognise, sitting up by the coach driver. "That's the organiser, Mr Dewdrop, from the Nice 'N' Neat Countryside

Alliance. It's their essay competition that Darius won—"

"That *I* won."

"Oh yes, whatever. But anyway, Mr Dewdrop is going to do a report on me this week. He'll judge me to see if I can get my Approved for Kids certificate. Should be easy. Kids love me; I'm totally down with them. I watch all the soaps they like and I can rap and everything."

"Please stop talking," said Nat.

"It'll be me getting top marks, obvs."

Dad plunked a few notes on his tiny little guitar.

"Although, just to be on the totally safe side, it would be great if you and your friends could tell Mr Dewdrop just how utterly brilliant you all think I am. All the time, every day, as often and as loudly as possible."

Nat groaned. It was so unfair. Not only was she expected to put up with her mega-embarrassing dad all week, but she was also supposed to say he was great! She wouldn't do it.

BUT another thought struck her. If Dad did well on this trip and then got his certificate, he could finally get a proper job *and be out of her hair…*

Dad pottered back to his seat at the front, trying to high-five the children as he went past. *No one* high-fived him back, so he pretended he was waving to passers-by outside. Someone outside waved back. Not nicely.

Nat cringed. It was going to be SO hard…

After a few hours, they were driving through yet another small soggy village, glistening and grey in the rain. Nat and Penny were sharing headphones, listening to Princess Boo's new album, and Darius was working on verse 768 of his epic poo poem, "Diarrhoea".

He kept pulling out Nat's earpiece, asking her to suggest rhymes for words like "squelchy" or "explode".

She was grateful for the interruption when Mr Dewdrop came and sat nervously by Darius.

Mr Dewdrop was a young man, very thin and pale, with ash-brown frizzy hair. He reminded Nat of a sickly reed, struggling for life in a marsh. He had encouraged a straggly moustache to cover up some of his red spots.

"Mr Bagley?" he said.

Darius looked around.

"He means you, idiot," said Nat.

"What?" Darius said dangerously. He didn't like strangers. He started shaking a can of fizzy pop and flicking at the ring pull as if to open it. It made Nat think of a rattlesnake shaking its tail, just as a casual warning.

"He doesn't like people sitting too close," said Nat, trying to be helpful, "although he *probably* won't bite."

Mr Dewdrop backed away and nervously checked a form he was carrying.

"Are you the Darius Bagley who wrote the prize-winning essay?" the young man said. "Or is there perhaps another Darius Bagley?" He sounded hopeful.

"That's him," said Penny, who was drawing fairies on a big sketch pad. "Have fun. And actually, Nathalia, he DOES bite."

"We're all very impressed with your hilarious essay," said Mr Dewdrop quickly. His voice was sometimes high and trembly, sometimes deep and croaky, like a frog playing a flute. Darius just stared. Mr Dewdrop ploughed on. "We'd like to give you free tickets to our new garden centre, in Lower Totley Village. You can get a half-price cream tea too. Yum."

Nat sniggered. She wasn't jealous of THAT rubbish prize. Darius looked at Mr Dewdrop blankly.

The young man coughed. "Right. And I hear you're team leader. So that means you get to stay in one of our luxury log cabins, with outdoor plunge pool and indoor table football."

"Get in!" yelled Darius, jumping up.

"Where do WE stay?" said Nat, who was suddenly jealous. Darius was making a big loser 'L' on his forehead at her.

"The rest of you will be in our cosy eco-yurts, made from natural – well, let's just say it's very natural. Don't worry about the goaty smell – you soon get used to it."

Darius burst out laughing, which lasted all the way to the next village, when Nat pinched him into silence.

"I looked up 'yurt'," said Penny. "I think it's like a tent, but not quite as good."

Flipping luxury log cabins for the flipping team

leader, thought Na[...] [...] way through the wet [...] *pool? So not fair.*

She stewed for a while, a[...] at Darius, "How come you get [...] and we have to live in rubbish tents n[...] goat bum?"

"Stop moaning. You get to bring your d[...]

Nat always forgot that Darius actually th[...] Dad was great. She had NO IDEA why.

"We're here," shouted Miss Hunny, before Nat could carry on her row.

The coach stopped dead with a squeal of old brakes.

Nat looked out of the window and just saw trees, dripping with rain. In the distance she thought she could see a sliver of grey sea.

"You might wanna put your macs on. There's a very light drizzle," shouted Dad, "or possibly only a sea mist."

The rain thrashed down harder. No one wanted to get out.

"It's a good job I'M here to keep everyone's spirits up," said Dad.

black

Keane,

's hail

s time

ıld go

it got.

ible. I

didn't

n and

putting his head in his hands. "Why didn't I work harder at school?" he cried.

No one quite knew what to say.

Finally, Miss Austen took charge. "Come on, children," she said bossily. "Last one off the coach is a Bagley."

"Hey," said Darius, as the stampede for the exit started.

They all ran helter-skelter from the coach towards the shelter of a large wooden hut in the middle of a clearing in the forest. Through the rain, from under her plastic hood, Nat could make out a sign reading:

Lower Totley Eco Camp

Parked next to the large hut was a gleaming-new white coach, with cool tinted windows and sleek curved lines. On it were emblazoned the golden words:

SAINT SCROFULA'S COLLEGE

And in smaller words underneath:

Gosh, what a great school!

Inside the smart coach, Nat caught a glimpse of a square-jawed driver in a uniform and peaked cap, watching a big TV screen. Then she heard a hacking cough behind her. It was their coach driver, Eric Scabb, sucking down on his first ciggy for two hours. He spat on a bush.

"Better out than in," he said.

Nat's coach had **SCABB'S BUDGET COACHES FOR HIRE** painted in flaking letters on the side.

"Their coach probably cost more than our entire school," Nat muttered to Penny, as they squished through the mud and into the wooden building.

Inside, the teachers went into a small reception area to fill out forms while Dad led the damp, hungry children into a large dining hall. It was full of long wooden tables and benches. And it was also full of other children, who stopped their chattering and stared at the newcomers.

The kids from the other school were those "sit-up-straight" kind of children. They were scrubbed clean and shiny and had smart blazers and even smarter haircuts. All the girls were blonde, Nat noticed, and not even slightly murky blonde like her, but almost white, dazzling blonde.

AND NOT ONE OF THEM ATE THEIR PEAS OFF THEIR KNIVES.

Nat looked at her wet, bedraggled, muddy classmates. *We look like survivors from a shipwreck*, she thought.

The other children continued to stare at Nat's class.

"You know in those cowboy films when they walk into the wrong saloon and it goes dead quiet?" Nat said to Darius. Then she thought for a minute. "Oh, I suppose you get that all the time, tee-hee," she said.

He glared at her.

There was a long, makeshift kitchen counter at one end of the hall, where two large ladies were splodging food on to wooden plates. Behind them bubbled cauldrons of something or other. From a distance it looked like brown porridge.

Rank brown porridge.

Nat's plan was to grab some food and sit somewhere away from the other kids as quietly and with as little fuss as possible. Which was pretty much the plan of everyone else in 8H too.

Except Dad.

Dad walked right slap bang into the middle of the dining hall and said, loudly, in his best 'down with the kids' kind of voice:

"Hey, dudes, how's it going down?"

Nat felt that familiar burning sensation trickle down the back of her neck.

"I'm Ivor," the big idiot continued, "but you can call me Mr Fun."

"Dad, stoppit," hissed Nat.

"Best to break the ice as soon as possible," said Dad cheerfully, while Nat tried to find a deep dark shadow to hide in.

Mr Fun turned to the perfect St Scrofula's children. "Anyone want to see a magic trick?"

"Yes, I think we'd all like to see you disappear,"

said a large boy with very short blond hair and startling blue eyes.

"We have a comedian," said Dad. "Ha ha, I love a bit of banter."

"Banter off, there's a good fellow," said Blue Eyes.

"As long as no one ever finds out he's my dad, I might be OK," Nat whispered to Penny.

"What's brown and sticky?" said Dad, trying out his favourite joke.

"A stick," said a bored blonde girl, who Nat reckoned was almost certainly called Jemima but who was actually called Plum.

"A stick," said Dad. "Oh, you guessed it!"

"He's an annoying little chap. Do you think we could pay him to go away?" said Blue Eyes.

"Oi, that's my dad you're talking about," Nat shouted angrily, stepping forward.

The shiny bright children from St Scrofula's turned to her and STARTED LAUGHING.

Oops, she thought. *I've gone and blown it already! This is gonna be a loooong week...*

CHAPTER FOUR

••••

NAT WAS WRONG. IT WAS A LONG *DAY*.

After a brown lunch of brown rice and brown lentils and brown bread, all the children were treated to a welcome talk by the owner and the team who ran the campsite.

The woman who owned Lower Snotley Eco Camp was called Mrs Ferret and she looked like a weasel. She had brown hair, sticky-out sharp teeth and little round glasses. She spoke so quickly and quietly that Nat had no idea what she was saying.

"I thought she said something about pooing in a hole in the ground," Nat whispered to Penny, who was looking deeply unhappy.

"I think she did," said Penny, "and then she said something about recycling everything."

"*Everything?*" said Nat, alarmed.

"I love it here." Darius grinned.

Mrs Ferret the weasel then introduced the man who ran all the outward-bound activities, a huge, leathery kind of fellow called Mr Bungee. Nat couldn't tell how old he was; she thought he'd just grown out of the ground like a tree. He was hard and bulgy, like a sock tightly stuffed with walnuts. Mr Bungee had a broad-brimmed leather hat decorated with sharks' teeth and a voice like a man on a mobile phone going through a long train tunnel.

"G'day, you little creatures," he shouted in a nasal twang. "I'm here to toughen you lot up. Get you used to the outdoor life. I'm gonna make men of the lot of you, eh?"

"Men? How about the girls?" said Nat, offended.

"ESPECIALLY the girls," said Mr Bungee.

"I bet you're brilliant at banter," said Dad, stepping forward.

Next to Mr Bungee, Dad didn't look like a sock filled with walnuts; he looked like a glove puppet filled with custard.

"Less banter, more action, that's what your blooming country needs," said Mr Bungee.

"Oooh, I think he's lovely," said Miss Austen, drooling a little.

"So do I, and I saw him first," said Miss Eyre.

"I can see you're a fair dinkum ocker, mate. G'day, Blue. How'd you do there, wallaby, to be sure," said Dad in a bizarre, strangulated accent. He sounded like a cross between a cowboy, a Jamaican, and someone involved in a road traffic accident.

"You feelin' all right?" said Mr Bungee.

"Yeah, kangaroo woologoroo koala," said Dad. "I'm just saying, I can tell you're an Australian. I'm dead good with accents. I'm a bit theatrical."

"You're a bit SOMETHIN' all right," said Mr B, "and I'll have you know I'm from NEW FLIPPING ZEALAND."

"Same thing, isn't it?" said Dad.

Mr Bungee went red. "Bit of a drongo, are you?" he said angrily. "Australians speak funny for a start, and they can't play rugby. Not that you'd know – you lot speak REALLY funny, and you're even

WORSE at rugby."

Everyone laughed at his joke, and Misses Eyre and Austen even gave him a round of applause.

Ew, thought Nat, *total suck-up alert.*

Mr Bungee picked up a list of names and read down it. "Ah, I know who you are," he said. "You must be Mr Bu—"

"Bew-mow-lay," shouted Nat, who knew how EVERYONE pronounced their hated surname.

"It says on my list that you've specially asked to be in charge of the entertainment, eh?" said Mr Bungee.

"I'm a born entertainer," said Dad.

"Well, you make me laugh all right," said Mr Bungee.

The St Scrofula's kids sniggered.

"Glad to help," said Dad, smiling.

Nat sighed.

"Now, I usually do the entertaining round here," said Mr Bungee, putting a thick arm around Dad, "but you know what they say at the urinals: there's always room for a little one!"

Dad smiled.

Nat DID NOT.

Her day didn't improve. Soon, Class 8H were shown to their "super" yurts.

So not super, thought Nat miserably, as she looked at the little round huts made of brown and yellow canvas and animal skin, propped up on bricks. Little coloured flags and ribbons fluttered from their ropes.

The rain had stopped but the campsite fields were still damp and muddy.

"All the stars have these yurt things when they go to festivals," said Penny brightly. "This is dead glamorous."

"They look like inflatable garden sheds," said Nat, "and there's nothing glamorous about a garden shed. Our local nutter, Plant Pot Pete, lives in a garden shed."

"You can imagine you're Princess Boo," said Penny, "just before a big concert."

"No, I can imagine I'm some mad old man in a string vest with a plant pot stuck on his head," grumbled Nat.

The biggest and best yurts were at the top of the slope, where the ground was less soggy and there was a lovely view over rolling green fields and out to sea. Annoyingly, those yurts had already been taken by the St Scrofula's kids.

The yurts at the bottom of the hill were near woods, were in permanent damp gloom, and the view was mostly of a pigsty. The *smell* was mostly of a pigsty too, but at least that covered up the smell of goat from the tents.

"Two to a yurt," said Miss Hunny. "Except Darius – you get a leader cabin with Rufus from St Scrofula's. Follow me."

"See you, Buttface," said Darius, leaving Nat behind.

She was more cross about him getting the nice cabin than she was about him dropping in her horrid nickname. (And it had taken her AGES to get him to use THAT name and not something far, far worse.)

Sulkily, Nat watched the leaders start up the hill. She stomped off and chucked her things into the dark yurt she'd be sharing with Penny.

"Which half of the floor do you want?" asked Penny kindly. "You can have the muddy, soggy half or the lumpy, rocky half."

"This isn't fair! I'm gonna see what the cheaty chimp Darius has got," said Nat, leaving.

She jogged jealously up the hill to watch as Darius and Rufus were shown to their smart log cabin nearby. It turned out that Rufus was the blue-eyed boy from St Scrofula's.

The two boys stood outside their cabin, eyeing each other.

Casually, Darius picked his nose and flicked it at Rufus. Rufus grabbed him and tried to bring him down, and the two of them went flying into the cabin. Miss Hunny closed the door on their bashing noises.

"Nothing to see here," she said, walking quickly past Nat. "Back to your yurt, please."

"I thought I was supposed to be looking after Darius," complained Nat.

A howl of pain floated towards them. It was Rufus.

"Oh, I'd say he's looking after himself right now," said Miss Hunny.

"Can't I have one of the nice cabins?" pleaded Nat.

"No special treatment, Nat. It wouldn't be fair,"

said Miss Hunny gently. "You're already super lucky because your dad's here. We don't want everyone getting jealous."

"No one who's met my dad is jealous of me," said Nat. "They either feel sorry for me or have a right good laugh."

Miss Hunny had a right good laugh.

"Your father always tells me how funny you are," she said, "and he's so right."

They walked past St Scrofula's nice yurts. Queen Bee of Year Eight, the amazing Flora Marling, was talking to Plum, the girl from St Scrofula's who had ruined Dad's joke.

This'll be interesting, thought Nat. The best six days of her school life so far had all involved Flora actually *talking to her*. Even if it had just been to ask Nat why on Earth she was friends with Darius Bagley.

Nat watched as Plum and Flora examined each other. Plum tossed her hair back; it was yellow in the pale sun. Then Flora flicked *her* hair and the sun broke through the clouds. All around Flora the air was golden. Plum gasped and Flora, victorious, smiled gracefully.

"Have my yurt," said the awestruck Plum, "please."

Flora smiled graciously then floated into the yurt, like a passing dream.

Nat trudged down the slope to the grotty yurts.

"You know, it could be really cosy in here," said Penny inside. "It just needs some brightening up."

"Brightening up?" Nat groaned, looking around her.

It was dark, damp and dismal.

"I wouldn't even mind, but we have actually invented hotels," grumbled Nat, unrolling her sleeping bag.

"You should be less grumbly and more proud of yourself," said Penny, whose favourite Princess Boo song was "Be More Proud of Yourself". She added, "Look on the bright side: if you hadn't written such a great essay, we wouldn't be getting a week off school."

"You're right," said Nat, cheering up. She squished a bug with her foot. "No school is good, you're right. I am pretty awesome, I suppose."

"And so modest," said Penny quietly.

"I just wish people would listen to me when I

try and tell them I wrote that essay," said Nat. "It would be nice to get some credit for something once in a while."

"OK, I promise that next time anyone mentions it, I'll definitely tell them it was you," said Penny.

Nat smiled. "Ta," she said. She looked around. "I *would* help you with the brightening-up, but I'm plotting how to get Bagley out of his cabin, and I need to concentrate."

She lay back on her sleeping bag and closed her eyes.

She was woken from her nap by Dad, who pottered in a little later. "Not too bad, is it?" he said.

Nat had already forgotten she had been cheered up. She wasn't going to miss a chance to complain at Dad. Somewhere, somehow, it was always his fault.

"Dad, the other school is horrible. The kids are rotten and spoiled and they've nicked all the best yurts. They ate all the pizza at lunch too, so we had to have slop. I think it was worms, and I'm not even joking."

"Mmm. Cracking good school though. Those children are just used to getting what they want.

Nothing wrong with that." He looked at Nat in a rather odd, thoughtful way. (It was odd *because* it was thoughtful.) "I've been chatting to the St Scrofula's teachers," he continued, "and they're all amazing. They're at school two hours early every day to organise extra lessons and activities."

"Yuk," said Nat.

"And next term they're going to extend school hours to seven o'clock at night."

"I'd feel sorry for them if they weren't so horrible," said Nat.

"Their last school play went to the West End, the head boy's going to be an astronaut, last year's sixth form are all doctors, and their football team are in the third round of the FA Cup."

"I'm not impressed," fibbed Nat, who was impressed.

"The head of media studies used to work on *Star Wars*, the head of art has a picture in the Tate Gallery, and guess who did their prize-giving? The flipping prime minister."

"Blimey," said Nat, "remember who did our prize-giving? Brian Futtock from Futtocks Coach Hire and Pest Control."

"Urgh, and all those rats got out," shuddered Penny, remembering the screams.

"Yeah, that was Darius," chuckled Nat. "He got a three-year detention – even broke his brother Oswald's school detention record."

"Maybe your mum's right," said Dad. "Maybe YOU should go to that school."

There was a horrible pause when Nat realised Dad wasn't joking.

"Don't even think about it," she said, going all hot and cold. "It's taken me ages to get to know THIS bunch of idiots. No offence, Penny." She turned to her friend.

"What was that?" said Penny, who was drawing a picture of Princess Boo, dressed as a fairy and riding on a unicorn, on the yurt wall.

"You writing that essay for Darius has done us a great favour," said Dad. "It's given us a chance to compare both schools, side by side."

Nat felt sick. She didn't want him to compare schools. Dad comparing the schools could be a DISASTER.

Dad left the yurt with a big smile on his face.

Behind him, Nat felt the familiar footsteps of

doom approaching. "I need some fresh air," she said, following him. "At least it smells nice out here."

"Time to dig the dunny!" yelled Mr Bungee, who was right outside.

CHAPTER FIVE

· · · ·

"WHO KNOWS WHAT A DUNNY *IS*?" ASKED Mr Bungee.

Children and teachers alike were assembled in a field near the camp. It had stopped raining and the sun was actually threatening to peek out.

Darius, who had a black eye, chuckled.

Rufus, who had TWO black eyes, was too busy scowling at Darius to answer.

"A dunny is what you need to dig today," shouted Mr Bungee, waving around a couple of heavy spades as if they were toothpicks. "In fact, you gotta dig two: one for boys and one for girls. Now can you guess?"

The quicker-brained children giggled.

"You gotta dig the dunnies nice and deep cos when you use them you don't want anything jumping up and biting you on your backside," he said. "That's a bit of a final clue, mates."

Nat had a horrible feeling she knew what a dunny was. She sidled over towards Dad. "Can I go home now please?" she said.

He just chuckled.

"Any volunteers to dig the dunnies?" screamed Mr Bungee.

No one moved.

"Thought so – there never are. So that's why we're gonna have a little healthy competition between your schools. The kids from the losing school will shovel the soil."

"That's not going to help the kids make friends," said Dad.

Mr Bungee looked at him like he was one of those bothersome spiders in a dunny.

"Friends?" he said. "I like to get a bit of rivalry going, and the dunny challenge is a great kick-starter."

"No, I think we're better off working together,"

said Dad. He had one eye on Mr Dewdrop, who had his notebook and clipboard out and was watching Dad closely.

"You're not in charge," said Mr Bungee.

"No one needs to be in charge," said Dad.

Nat looked across at Mr Dewdrop, who frowned and scribbled a big 'X' in his book. *Uh-oh*.

"But maybe they do need to be in charge," said Dad, seeing the cross and changing his mind quickly. "Well said. Carry on."

Nat sighed.

Mr Keane, their gloomy geography teacher, raised his head. "We should really do a survey on the best place to site a dunny," he said. Then he groaned. "That's using geography, that is. That's what it's for. Depressing, isn't it?"

Nat heard some grown-up snooty sniggering. There were three St Scrofula's teachers standing there, and they were all at it. It was the first time Nat had had a good look at them.

They were all bright and shiny and correct, like the buttons on a soldier's tunic. They were annoyingly tall, annoyingly smart, and annoyingly impressive. She had hoped they would be a little bit rubbish like all her teachers. But of course they weren't. It was annoying.

Just by looking at them, Nat knew Dad would approve, which was even more annoying.

While Mr Keane pulled himself together, the new teachers introduced themselves to Nat's class.

There was a Dr Nobel, who taught science, and had tiny, round, shiny glasses and a big, round, shiny head.

There was a Miss Slippy, who taught advanced geography and was as thin as a toothpick.

And there was a Mr Rainbow, who was completely and totally grey. He taught difficult science, advanced chemo-biology and something about time travel, but Nat had given up listening by then to be perfectly honest.

They were all the smartly-dressed, scrubbed-clean, shiny-shoed, sharp-eyed kind of teacher. Not one of them was covered in tea stains, bean juice and despair, like Mr Keane.

Nat saw Dad study the super trio carefully, before looking at her crumpled, unhappy geography teacher. He then stared at the irritating Misses Austen and Eyre, whose classes regularly got the worst exam results in the county.

Nat could see exactly what Dad was thinking. Convincing him that her school was the best was going to be an uphill struggle.

"Are all your teachers like these two?" Mr Bungee asked Miss Hunny, indicating Dad and Mr Keane. "Funny sort of school, isn't it?"

The kids from St Scrofula's giggled.

"There's nothing funny about my school," said Miss Hunny, offended.

Now it was Nat's class's turn to laugh.

But Nat didn't laugh. She was looking at Dad's face. He was wearing the only expression that ever scared her.

Dad was taking it all in... HE WAS THINKING.

He was looking at the bright, shiny faces of the St Scrofula's kids. He was thinking that they were WINNERS. And pretty soon, Nat realised, he was going to want his little princess to be a St Scrofula's winner too.

Right, thought Nat, *these rotten winner kids will just have to start losing. And they have to start losing RIGHT NOW.*

She looked at the spades.

And THERE'S NO WAY we're digging their flipping dunny.

The Who's Digging the Dunny? competition took place in the field.

"Each school chooses one representative to take part," shouted Mr Bungee. "It's a test of brains."

"Flora Marling," shouted Nat's class.

"And it's a test of strength."

"Marcus Milligan," shouted Nat's class.

"And it's so dangerous you might never see them again."

"Darius Bagley," shouted Nat's class.

"I'm only pulling your legs about the danger, campmates," laughed Mr Bungee.

"Oh," said Nat's class, disappointed.

"That man's so very amusing," trilled Miss Austen, "as well as being a dreamboat."

"A born comedian," said Miss Eyre.

"We've got Ivor," said Miss Hunny, indicating her hilarious old college friend, Dad.

"I think you mean we've got a jester," sniffed Miss Austen.

"Or a village idiot," sniffed Miss Eyre.

"Is it true?" said Mr Keane, who'd missed the last few minutes because he'd been crying in a ditch. "Is it really so dangerous you might not return? I want to volunteer. Please let me."

"It's not enough that everyone in my family is potty," Nat said to Penny, "or that everyone I know is barking mad. It just has to be all my teachers too!"

"What do you mean, everyone you know is mad?" said Penny, who was holding a Y-shaped stick out in front of her.

"I didn't include you," said Nat, who totally did include Penny. "What are you doing?"

"Looking for ley lines. It's like magic energy. This campsite's built on an ancient burial ground. I read it somewhere. "

Nat decided she really needed to make better friends.

She watched as Darius, standing on his own, practised his long-distance spitting, and noticed how he was cleverly using the wind to get some curl.

She decided she REALLY needed to make better friends.

Darius grinned at her and she grinned back. Then she remembered she was still cross with him.

She marched up to him, ready for pinching. He backed away.

"It's so not fair you get a nice chalet, even if you do have to share with that stuck-up Rufus."

"Not any more," said Darius. "He left. Said he prefers a yurt."

"Why don't *you* say that too, and I can have your chalet?" said Nat. "It's only cos of me that we're here."

"Get lost," said Darius. "*I* don't prefer a yurt."

Nat was about to pinch him when she saw Miss Hunny watching. She patted Darius like a dog.

"Nice Darius, good Darius," she said, remembering she was supposed to be looking after him.

"I'm confused now," said Darius, who'd been expecting pinching.

He ran off anyway, to be on the safe side.

Mr Bungee was shouting again.

"The team leaders have five minutes to choose their dunny champion," he said, "so get a move on."

Nat spent the next five minutes arguing with Penny about how stupid ley lines were, and so she hardly noticed Dad having a long conversation with Darius. She probably should have paid more attention because what happened next took her completely by surprise.

"Nathalia is our dunny champion," said Miss Hunny. "And it was a fair vote, so don't start arguing."

"How did this happen? No one even mentioned me. Have YOU done this, Dad?" she said angrily.

He took her to one side.

"Shush," he said. "I don't want Mr Dewdrop from the Nice 'N' Neat Alliance to think I'm pulling strings for you. It's not very professional."

"You haven't pulled strings. You've DROPPED ME IN IT! There's a massive difference. Why have you done this?" she complained.

"I know you're always worried about making friends and being popular," said idiot Dad kindly, "so what better way than by being the class champion?"

"Class DUNNY champion."

"A winner's a winner."

"What if I lose?" she said. "It'll be *my* fault my classmates are digging the dunny."

"Don't be so negative," said Dad with his lopsided smile. "Honestly, sometimes I think I've got more confidence in you than you do."

Nat was told to get changed into something "she didn't mind getting a bit muddy", which alarmed her. She stomped back to the half-dark yurt and rummaged around in her rucksack in the gloom until she found an old T-shirt and a pair of tracky bottoms.

On her way back down the hill, she began to think. Maybe... just maybe Dad had done her a favour. Perhaps this *was* her chance to get one over on St Scrofula's stuck-up school. If she could win... well, maybe her school wouldn't seem so bad after all.

IF she could win.

CHAPTER SIX

· · · ·

"Can we have the competitors?" said Mr Bungee. "Get a move on. No one wants to be digging a dunny in the dark."

Nat trudged over to the enthusiastic Kiwi.

Her opponent was Plum, who had actually volunteered herself for the challenge.

"I'm not being big-headed," said large-bonced Plum, "I just know I'm smart and fast and super able."

"There you go," said Dad, "that's what I call confidence. What a school!"

"Shuddup, Dad," said Nat.

"There are three rounds," said Mr Bungee, "so

the first girl to win two rounds is the winner."

"Get on with it," snapped Nat.

"The first round is a general-knowledge quiz," said Mr Bungee. "So, what's the capital of New Zealand?"

"Italy," guessed Nat, who was pants at geography.

"Wellington," said Plum.

"Wellington it is," said Mr Bungee. "And a bloomin' lovely place it is too, eh?"

The St Scrofula's kids cheered.

"Next question. Cuddly little koala bears are native to Australia – and they're the only good thing about the place, if you ask me. Now, what do they eat?"

"Bugs. Or grass or toast," guessed Nat.

"Wrong."

"Or milk, fish, bread, eggs, cheese…"

"Way off."

"Pies. Peanuts. Ready-salted crisps. Sweet popcorn. Chicken nuggets."

"Stop guessing."

"Eucalyptus leaves," said Plum smugly.

"Correct," said Mr Bungee. "Next question. Who's the queen of New Zealand?"

"This isn't general knowledge," complained Nat.

"It's general knowledge to me," said Mr Bungee.

"Is it Kylie?" said Nat.

"NO. Firstly, Kylie's a pop princess. Secondly, she's another Aussie. You're worse than your father."

"It's actually a really clever question," said Plum, with a smarmy smile. "You haven't really got a queen, but because you're in the Commonwealth, you share ours."

"How do you KNOW this stuff?" said Nat, who wanted to throttle her rival.

"It's called an education," said Plum.

Nat scowled.

She looked at Dad. He looked impressed.

"You have to admit it: they're making us look like idiots, love," he said.

"St Scrofula's wins the first round," said Mr Bungee, to cheers from one lot of kids and boos from the other.

"The second round is an eating challenge. First rule of camp survival: you gotta eat."

He dangled two fat chilli peppers in front of the girls.

"We call these the Auckland Bum-burners. They

are hot. Hot enough to boil a kiwi's behind. The first one to eat a whole chilli wins."

With relief, Nat saw that Plum looked nervous.

Nat took a pepper. It almost glowed red in her hand, like an ember from a fire.

She looked at her classmates. They were all urging her on. If Nat lost this, they would lose the contest. She had no choice. She rammed the thing in her mouth and started chewing.

It wasn't too bad for about half a nanosecond.

Then it was bad. Very bad indeed.

Nat thought the roof of her mouth was going to erupt through the top of her head. Her tongue felt like a firework and even her teeth rattled.

"I'M GOING TO DIE AND I'M NOT EVEN JOKING!" she yelled, running around in circles, mouth open, desperately trying to suck in cooling air.

"WATER, WATER, GIMME WATER!!!!"

She snatched Penny's water bottle and took huge gulps.

"Water makes it worse," said Mr Bungee, with a nasty grin.

"AAAAGH, YOU COULD HAVE TOLD ME

EARLIER!" Nat screamed, running around some more, tongue hanging out like a thirsty dog.

It took about five minutes for the throbbing pain to die down, and about ten minutes for everyone to stop laughing at her.

"Did I win?" Nat said finally. Her eyes streamed with tears and she could hardly speak.

"Course you won," said Plum in a superior kind of way. "I didn't do it."

"Why not?" asked Nat.

"Didn't need to – I was already one up. I'll wait for the third challenge."

"Tiebreaker," said Mr Bungee. "Winner takes all. Loser takes… a couple of dunny shovels."

"Ooooh," said the watching kids from both schools, who were now all willing their champion to victory. And wishing poo-shaped defeat on their rivals.

"We think you're awesome, Plum," shouted her best friend, a tall girl called Thursday Wonton. "Absolutely amazeballs."

"Yay!" cheered the Scrofulas.

"You'd better win, Buttface," said Darius helpfully. "You're unpopular enough as it is."

"Yay," agreed Nat's class.

Nat scowled at them.

Mr Bungee, who was milking the suspense for all it was worth, finally made the announcement they were waiting for.

"The last challenge is a straightforward race," he said.

It was straightforward. Straight and forward through an assault course.

The huge assault course was already set up in the woods. There were ropes to swing along, a net to crawl under, a pipe to squeeze through, tyres to hop in and out of, and then, finally, a big wooden wall.

"Best thing is, all the mud will break your fall," said Mr Bungee, "so you can really go for it. Are you ready?"

"No. Not really," said Nat unhappily.

But Mr Bungee had already raised a whistle to his lips.

"There's a bell on a tree at the end of the course," he said. "The first one to ring it wins."

All the kids yelled as he blew for the start of the race.

Plum was off like a rocket, squishing through the mud.

The first obstacle was a big net, close to the ground. Nat watched as her rival slid under it with practised ease.

"You've done this before," said Nat, as she got to the net.

"Yah, we've got our own assault course at school," said Plum, who was halfway through. "It's so fun."

So fun, yah. The only assault course we've got is running past the Year Eleven boys smoking behind the science block, thought Nat grimly, as she dived under the net after her opponent.

The mud was cold and sticky and soon she was plastered in it. But before Nat could wiggle out the other side, Plum was already whizzing along the monkey bars like, well, like a monkey.

"You're losing!" shouted Penny from the sidelines.

"Tell me something I don't know," said Nat, reaching the monkey bars.

"Your tracky bottoms are coming loose," said Penny, telling her something she didn't know.

"EEEK!"

Automatically, Nat put her hands down to pull up her trousers. Forgetting she was holding on to the monkey bars.

Splat! Down she went, into the mud.

"You fall off, you gotta start again," shouted Mr Bungee.

Nat squelched desperately back to the start of the course and began again.

Halfway across, going hand-to-hand on the bars, she became aware of her problem tracky bottoms. Why *were* they so loose? She kept crossing her skinny legs to hold them up, but they kept slipping down!

"I think I mixed up our tracky bottoms and I packed mine in your rucksack by mistake," shouted Dad. "They might be a bit big for you." He fidgeted on the spot. "Also, it might explain why I've got a bit of chafing. I thought these were tight."

"We can see your pa-ants!" chanted the boys from St Scrofula's. "We can see your pa-ants!"

Dangling there in mid-air, covered in mud and with Dad's oversized tracky bottoms sliding down, Nat heard a horrible wail of fury. She wondered

where it was coming from. Then she realised: it was coming from her!

She saw Dad – rubbish, tracky-bottoms-swapping, pants-revealing Dad – standing at the end of the assault course. He waved.

A red mist descended in front of her eyes.

This time she WAS GOING TO STRANGLE HIM.

With a yell, she raced through the monkey bars, hurled herself into the pipe, hopped furiously across the tyres and reached the big wall just as Plum was disappearing over it.

"Come 'ere, you," she shouted, and grabbed Plum's leg.

"Aaaargh!" yelled the girl, as Nat yanked her off the wall and used her as a stepping stone.

Nat was over the wall and in the lead! She was

way ahead. Nothing could stop her now.

"You've won, now ring the bell," yelled Dad.

But then he saw that Nat DID NOT CARE ABOUT THE BELL.

She was completely ignoring the bell.

Instead, she was heading straight for him, outstretched hands full of gooey mud.

"I'll just… just go and, er… look for something in these trees," said Dad, ducking behind a handy oak.

"You've embarrassed me for the last time," shouted Nat, chasing him in circles.

She had just got him cornered against a big tree and was about to plaster him in mud when she heard a bell ring.

It was Plum, ringing in victory.

"Oops," said Nat.

CHAPTER SEVEN

• • • •

IN THE END, DAD DUG THE DUNNY.

Nat said he had to because it was his fault she'd lost the race. If she hadn't been so cross with him, she'd have made it to the bell on time.

While the camp cooks were boiling up sludge for supper, Nat and Penny and Darius went to the field to see how Dad was getting on.

Nat was planning to offer words of encouragement like: "Hurry up, baldy," or "Dig it a bit deeper. We don't want spiders or splashback."

Darius just wanted to go so he could use it first.

When they got there, they could just see Dad's bald spot peeking above ground. There was a mound of freshly-dug earth near the hole. Great shovelfuls of earth were being chucked up... and over Mr Dewdrop, who was standing next to the hole.

"Are you sure you're setting a good example to the children?" Nat heard Mr Dewdrop ask, brushing earth off his clipboard. "I mean, you should get your girl Nathalia to do it. After all, it's usually 'losers, weepers', everyone knows that."

"Thanks. You could have said that two hours ago," grumbled Dad, climbing out, covered in mud and dirt and worms. "I've finished it now."

Darius whipped out some loo roll. "Out of my way," he said with an evil grin.

Dad just smiled. "We need to put the little loo hut over it first," he said. "Here, you can give me a hand."

After a few minutes of heaving and dragging (Darius and Dad) and groaning and complaining (Nat), they had manoeuvred the little loo hut over the big hole.

Mr Dewdrop wandered off without helping and Nat had a horrible feeling Dad wasn't making a good impression on him.

Darius dashed straight inside the dunny.

Dad brushed himself down and looked at the pile of earth he'd dug up. "I was hoping to find a bit of T. rex in the ground," he said. "There's tons of fossils round here."

Nat, who didn't care about fossils, just grunted.

Dad pointed to the pile of earth. "But all I found were three tin cans, something you don't need to know about, and this rock."

He showed Nat and Penny his lump of rock.

Nat was even less interested in rock than fossils, but Penny said, "Ooh, pretty."

She held it in her hand. Mostly it was grey and sharp and knobbly. But bits of it sparkled gold.

"Don't get too excited, it's only pyrite," said Dad.

"That's nice," said Penny.

"So bored," said Nat.

"It's called fool's gold," said Dad, "because lots of fools think it's gold. Apparently the ground here is full of it."

"Whatevs," said Nat. "Do you know you can't get a phone signal round here? All week, Dad, *with no phone signal*. Not even no Wi-Fi, but NO SIGNAL."

But Dad was still more interested in his glittery

rock. "Can you imagine, spending all that time and effort digging for this, only to be told, when it's finally in your hand, it's worthless?" he chuckled. "There's a life lesson in that somewhere but I can't remember what it is."

"There's no life lesson. It's totally pointless, a bit like you," snapped Nat.

She snatched the rock from Penny and hurled it over a hedge.

A cow mooed.

"Oops, sorry," she said.

"What's the matter with you?" said Penny, as Dad went to check on the well-being of the unfortunate cow.

"I'll tell you what. I've just been humiliated in my pants, my dad's had to dig a poo-hole, we're surrounded by the snooty kids from snooty-land, somehow I've gotta prove that our rubbish school is better than St flipping Scrofula's, we're going to be sleeping in a damp yurt in a damp field and, worst of all, Darius flipping Bagley is in a luxury chalet living like the Sultan of China."

"China doesn't have sultans," corrected Darius from inside the hut.

"Whatevs," grumbled Nat. "And then Dad starts burbling about a pointless rock that only *looks* like gold."

In the distance, a dinner bell clanged.

"Oh, bum-wads," swore Darius, who was still busy.

"Can I have your chalet?" said Nat for the zillionth time.

"Get lost and save me some slop," he demanded.

"Have fun in your new chalet," Nat yelled.

Grabbing a big branch from the ground, she wedged it tight against the dunny door, locking her little monster mate inside.

"Yeah, this one suits you better," she chortled.

Dinner was a kind of stew; actually, it was more of an *unkind* of stew because it bubbled and gurgled in Nat's tummy before she'd finished it. It was served in rough wooden bowls.

"Apparently the kids who were here last week made the bowls," said Penny, picking a splinter out of her tongue.

"Could this place get any worse?" said Nat, five minutes before IT GOT WORSE.

She budged up on her bench to make way for Darius, arriving late. He scowled at her.

"I had to climb out of the top," he said.

"Tee-hee," said Nat, handing him her leftover stew, "you should let me have the cabin, shouldn't you?"

When dinner was cleared away, Mr Dewdrop got up on a little wooden stage at the end of the hall. He looked a mixture of really self-important and terrified.

Nat noticed Dad was sitting right in front of Mr Dewdrop, with that stupid expression that reminded her of their dog, begging for scraps. '*I'm a good boy*,' he was basically saying. Dad just needed a flipping tail.

Mr Dewdrop clapped his hands together.

The well-behaved posh kids immediately paid attention; 8H carried on chatting/chucking bits of bread around/hunting for splinters.

Finally, they were brought to order.

"I'd like to welcome the best young geographers in the county," he said.

Everyone in 8H looked around to see who was walking in, but Nat realised he meant THEM.

"Congratulations to both schools on making it this far in the competition," Mr Dewdrop continued.

THIS FAR? thought Nat. *Competition? I thought the essay-writing was the competition.*

"As you know, as the winners of our essay prize, we've organised this lovely week in Totley for you, thanks to Mrs Ferret and Mr Bungee and their great eco camp."

Small applause.

"But that's only just the start. It's not all fun and games, as you know."

"There's not been ANY fun and games so far," said Julia Pryde.

"Ha ha, very funny. Wrong attitude, so stop it," said Mr Dewdrop. "There's going to be another competition while you're here. Your teachers should have had all the details on email last week."

Miss Hunny looked pained. She coughed, sounding apologetic. "Actually, our school didn't pay the last broadband bill, so our Internet's been cut off. Could you just tell us what you mean by another competition?"

Nat groaned. Even her *school* was embarrassing. But no one else from 8H even noticed, mainly because no one else was listening. They were watching Darius hang upside down from the back of a chair.

"We sent a letter to both the essay winners," said Mr Dewdrop. He looked at Darius. "Didn't you get it?"

"The postman doesn't deliver to Darius's house," explained Nat. "He's a bit nervous."

Mr Dewdrop smiled a forced smile. "The winners of the essay competition, with the help of their classmates, will take part in another competition. They need to present a big geography project on Saturday. It's carnival day in Lower Totley and announcing the winner will be part of the fantastic entertainment!"

"What sort of project will it be?" said Miss Hunny.

"It's going to be so exciting," trilled Mr Dewdrop. "The children have to make something based on what we do here this week. There'll be loads of bonus marks for the school that goes the extra mile – or kilometre, as we now say. Basically, you can't work too hard!"

"Wanna bet?" said Marcus Milligan.

"Just make sure you celebrate our green and pleasant countryside!" said Mr Dewdrop.

"Wanna see something green and *un*pleasant?" said Darius. "Just look in my snot rag."

Nat saw Mr Dewdrop shudder. She grinned. She reckoned the employees of the Nice 'N' Neat Countryside Alliance weren't used to schools like hers.

But then she saw Dad frowning. *Oops*, she thought.

Mr Dewdrop ploughed on. "Isn't that exciting?"

"You are so lame," moaned Julia Pryde.

Nat giggled.

"I thought this was a holiday," said Milly Barnacle. "Holiday camp, they said."

"Yeah, but now we've got to work to make the project," moaned Marcus Milligan. "Stupid projects."

"And present it in front of the whole town," moaned Sally Bung.

"Blame Bagley," said Julia Pryde. "For winning the poxy essay competition in the first place."

"Yeah, I can't wait to see him up on stage presenting our work," said Peaches Bleary.

All of 8H laughed.

Until Darius spoke.

"I'm not doing it," said Darius. He pointed at Nat. "SHE wrote the essay. It's her fault."

"It IS her fault," said Miss Hunny.

"That's right," said Dad. "She worked really hard on that essay so give her the credit."

"So NOW I get the credit?" said Nat.

"Yes, you get the credit," said Penny, suddenly remembering her promise. "Listen, everyone, it's all Nathalia's doing." She smiled at Nat.

The rest of 8H were glaring at her.

"Is this true?" said Mr Dewdrop. "Did you write that wonderful essay?"

Nat stood up and sighed. "Yes," she admitted.

"Oh," Mr Dewdrop said, "this is most irregular. But everything is organised. Changing things now would cause a lot of mess. So, well, *you'll* have to present your class project, that's all."

All of 8H were now laughing at Nat.

"What?" said Nat. "Not fair. Have you seen my class? I'll look like an idiot." She looked at her classmates. "No offence."

But Mr D had started so he was going to finish.

"You'll present your projects at our headquarters, the former library, at Lower Snotley – I mean, Lower Totley – on Saturday. The mayor will be there, and the local paper. And the school whose work is judged the best will get... a cup!"

"Ooh," went the super-keen St Scrofula's kids.

Nat's class just made rude noises.

"And not just a cup," said Mr Dewdrop. "Your school will get a packet of garden centre coupons too!"

Now 8H started laughing at *him*.

Mr Dewdrop looked confused, but then Nat nudged the chair Darius was rocking on and Darius fell on his head.

NOW they cheered.

Mr Dewdrop smiled, thinking they were cheering him and his competition. He sat down, grateful it was over.

Dad leapt to his feet and clapped a hand on Nat's shoulder. "That's brilliant news," he said. "I'm sure you'll do ever so well making the project and presenting it." He nodded towards her classmates and teachers and lowered his voice. "And anyway, winning's not everything, is it?

CHAPTER EIGHT

· · · ·

THERE WAS A SHOWER BLOCK NEARBY, HOUSED IN a long building made of brick.

"What was the point of digging our own loo?" grumbled Nat, showering under a feeble stream of lukewarm water. "They've got loads of flipping loos in here."

She was talking to Penny in the next cubicle, but from the other side of her shower stall came Plum's snooty voice:

"We're learning valuable life lessons. Don't you know anything?"

"What possible life lesson can you learn from digging your own poo-hole?" snapped Nat, trying to get her soap to lather.

"How about not winning stupid camping prizes you don't want?" said Penny, just loud enough for Nat to hear.

Just before bed, the children were told to gather around a big campfire. Mrs Ferret said it was something to do with "bonding".

Nat had no intention of "bonding" with the St Scrofula's lot, so had to be practically dragged there by Penny, who hoped there'd be spooky ghost stories.

But when she got to the big crackling fire, Nat found it was WAY MORE FRIGHTENING than silly ghost stories.

DAD WAS PLAYING THE UKULELE!

IN FRONT OF EVERYONE!!

Noooo, she thought.

Dad was sitting

on a log, enjoying every second of the attention.

"I'm a teller of tales," he said, plunking away, "a singer of songs, a weaver of dreams."

"A massive embarrassment…" muttered Nat.

"I'm the bard of bad, the balladeer of being down."

"There's so many meteorites in the universe," Nat said to Darius, who she noticed HAD NOT HAD A SHOWER, "you'd think just one could whizz down and land on me. Or better still, Dad. But they never ever do."

Darius grinned. In the firelight he looked demonic. Mind you, considered Nat, Darius would look like a demon even if he worked in a tea shop run by two retired vicars and a fluffy cat called Mr Snuffles.

"It's getting late," said Nat, prodding him with a smoky stick. "Last chance to give me your chalet. Or there shall be… consequences."

Darius looked at her, a faint smile on his grubby face.

"Like what?" he said.

"I can think of terrible things," she said. "Just not right at this second."

"Enjoy the yurt," said Darius, dodging out of pinching range.

Just then, Mr Bungee came over to the fire, carrying something that looked like a big green nest. He sat by Dad and put a friendly arm around him.

"You're doing a great job with the entertaining, eh?" said Mr Bungee, with what Nat thought was a crafty smile. "I bin doing a lot of thinking about you."

"That's nice," said Dad. "The only thing worse than being thought about is NOT being thought about."

"I was thinking you're just what this camp needs."

"Glad you noticed," said Dad happily. He looked sideways at Mr Dewdrop and gave him a quick thumbs-up.

"You're like the real spirit of the woods, I reckon," said Mr B.

"That's what I've been saying," said Dad. "I am the teller of tales and the weaver of dreams, the oracle of the oak and the bard of the birch."

Nat groaned; Dad always got so carried away. But Mr Bungee was clapping Dad on the back.

"You're like our very own Green Bogey."

"Come again?" said Dad, who suddenly sounded less than impressed.

"Everyone around here knows about the Green Bogey. A Green Bogey is like a woodland sprite, or playful spirit," said Mr B. "Green Bogeys are everywhere."

"Yeah – look, I've caught loads," said Darius, showing Nat his hanky.

"Gerroff," she said, hitting him, "you've done a snot joke once today already."

"Hmm. Well, that sounds sensible enough," said Dad. "What does the Green Bogey do?"

"Same great fun stuff you're doing now," said Mr B, "except you do it… in the Green Bogey hat. I made it specially for you."

He produced the most ridiculous thing to go on a head since the invention of the combined baseball cap and clock radio Dad had once bought out of a catalogue.

It was made from green willow branches and covered with twigs and leaves and bits of grass. Worse, there were bells inside, which tinkled as Mr Bungee plopped it on to Dad's head.

"Careful of the thinning bit," said Dad, "that tickles."

It was a horrible, ridiculous mess.

If the Bagleys were birds, that's the nest they'd make, thought Nat.

Dad turned to the children, who were now oddly quiet.

"So what do you think?" he said, shaking his head so the leaves rustled and the bells tinkled. "I'm the Green Bogey!"

Nat thought the laughter that followed would never end.

But sadly it did end, because Dad had something he wanted to share with everyone.

A SONG.

"I'm writing the saga of your great camping adventure this week," said Dad, "and each night, I will sew more stories into the woof and warp of the tapestry of the, er, no, it's more the... the cloth of, um, perhaps the woolly blanket of your... Oh, I think I've lost my train of thought somewhere. I was definitely weaving. Or sewing."

"Get on with it," said Rufus from the safety of the darkness beyond the firelight.

"Good point, that, man," said Dad. "I shall now get on with it. This is called 'Green Bogey Man Boogie'."

He plucked a few dodgy chords on his ukulele, cleared his throat, and started to sing.

Well, not sing, exactly, but he began to make a noise. Dad sang the way a hippopotamus belly dances. That is, very badly and often with fatal results.

"I'm the green man from the forest," sang Dad,
"And everything is green,
My head is green, my feet are green,
And everything in between is green, oh,
And everything in between."

"And everything in between," sang the children, in between their giggles.

A few of the ruder boys demonstrated what kind of "in between" they thought Dad meant.

But Dad, who loved an audience, especially when they were laughing, thought he was a big hit and carried on warbling.

"I look after all the doves," he wailed, getting a bit carried away,
"I look after all the bunnies,

I put on rubber gloves, oh,
And then dig all the dunnies.
And then dig all the dunnies."

"*And then dig all the dunnies, oh,*" sang all the kids, minus Nathalia. She was edging towards a nice, thick, leafy, dark bush.

It can't possibly get worse, she thought.

But then it got worse.

"*Well, the wind, it was a-blowin',*
And the grass, it was a-growin',
And the cattle were a-lowin',
And Nathalia's pants were a-showin'
On the monkey bars, oh,
On the monkey bars."

That was it. The camp erupted with laughter. Even Dad's old friend Miss Hunny had shoved a hanky in her mouth, but she couldn't stop her shoulders shaking.

"Dad, shut up!" shouted Nathalia, but her words were drowned out by the laughter.

She jumped up and stamped her foot in shame and fury. Which only made the laughter worse. Coldly she marched over to Dad and snatched his wretched ukulele off him.

"Be a good sport, love," said Dad quickly, looking backwards and forwards between his angry daughter and the campfire, which was too near his little instrument for comfort. "There's loads more verses. Everyone in the camp comes in for a bit of gentle ribbing."

He lowered his voice. "I can't leave you out – it'll look like favouritism."

Nat drew her arm back as if to lob the hated uke into the flames. Dad hopped up and grabbed it off her.

"Careful," he said, "that's the spanner of the gods."

"No, Dad, YOU'RE the spanner of the gods," she said, stomping off.

She glared at Mr Dewdrop, who was scribbling with a pencil on his big stupid clipboard, as always.

"What are YOU looking at?" she snarled.

He coughed nervously. "Are you part of the act?" he said.

A red mist came down in front of Nat's eyes. She grabbed his pencil and hurled it into the flames.

"Yes I am," she said, "and that's the big finish."

As she stormed off, she heard Dad's voice.

"I think that school's having a bad influence on her," he was saying. "I've noticed she does get very cross these days and that's the only sensible explanation."

AAAAGH, thought Nat.

"That snobby school is making us a laughing stock," said Nat. "And my dad doesn't need any help with that."

She was lying in her sleeping bag, wide awake, in her horrid yurt with Penny. It was the middle of the night and light from her phone was casting spooky shadows on the cloth walls. Outside owls hooted and somewhere a cow mooed. They seemed a million miles from anywhere.

Over in his cabin, Darius farted so loudly it sent the owl flapping off with a shriek. And it woke Penny with a start.

"What? Oh, they're not *all* bad," yawned Penny. "I met a nice girl called Perudo Box today. She's got pet llamas and she says I can visit and feed them and everything."

"Ooh, you big fat traitor," said Nat.

"Why do you hate on them so much?" said Penny,

who didn't hate on anything. Which Nat hated.

"Because my stupid dad thinks the sun shines out of their exam results," said Nat. "And now they're gonna look awesome on Saturday. They'll come up with some mega project to show off when we haven't even had a single idea yet. And let's face it, all I know about geography is how to dig a dunny."

"You've got us and Mr Keane to help you come up with an idea for a winning project," said Penny. "Doesn't that sound good?"

Nat just groaned.

The big worry in Nat's mind swam to the surface and raced away. "I'm gonna make a right fool of myself, with all your help. Then Dad's gonna think I need to be at a better school and *then* he'll send me there. What happens THEN?"

"You'd probably get more than twelve per cent in your biology tests, for a start," said Penny, who was just being honest.

"I revised the wrong things, stop going on about it," said Nat. "Look, I'm not going to that school." She thought hard. "Which means, they need to look as rubbish as us."

"So what are you going to do to them?" yawned

Penny, closing her eyes.

"Dunno. Normally I'd just get Darius to come up with an evil plan, but I'm not talking to him because he won't let me have the chalet."

"Ask your other friends then."

Nat wasn't sure she had that many. She ticked off the options on her fingers: "Julia Pryde's quite a meanie, which could be useful but I don't really trust her. Sally Puddle is a total teacher's pet even though she, like, pretends she isn't—"

"OMG, she so is," agreed Penny.

"Don't interrupt. Peaches Bleary is one of those girly girls. And the only other girl I'm sort of friends with is Milly Barnacle and I don't like her anyway. She's a bit clingy."

There was a long pause.

In the dark, Penny said, "There's me. I can help."

"Yeah, right," said Nat.

"What does that mean?" said Penny.

If Nat hadn't been quite so wrapped up in herself, she might have noticed Penny sounded a bit hurt.

"You're a total goody two-shoes," said Nat. "I need someone who can be devious and evil and sneaky. And not someone who thinks they're a fairy princess from the cloud city of la-la land. No offence."

"I am offended, actually," said Penny, but into her sleeping bag so Nat wasn't sure she'd heard her right.

Nat closed her eyes and waited for sleep. She had heard that great lungfuls of fresh air and dollops of exercise and lashings of good wholesome food make you sleep like a top.

Still wide awake hours later, she wanted to find the idiot who said that and throttle them.

CHAPTER NINE

····

"SLEEP ALL RIGHT?" NAT ASKED DARIUS THE next morning.

She was REALLY grumpy.

They were in the dining room, shovelling down heaped plates of fried stuff. Dad was helping out with the cooking, which was a shock for most people who liked normal food. Nat was used to the greasy, burned mess that stared back at her from her tin plate. Going by the retching sounds from the St Scrofula's kids, she guessed they were used to rather finer grub.

"Did you have a nice, long, relaxing slumber in your luxury cabin of loveliness?" said Nat, bouncing her fork off a rubber egg.

"Can't remember, I was too busy being asleep," said munching Darius, who ate anything. And was, as usual, eating with his mouth open.

"I feel sick," said a St Scrofula's girl sitting opposite, called Tallulah Puddleduck.

"Wanna know how my night was?" hissed Nat.

Behind her, Dad was waving a tea towel at a smoking frying pan.

"Nope," said Darius, grabbing a bottle of ketchup and squirting it into his mouth. Some dribbled out of his nose. He reached it with his tongue.

"I feel sick too," said another St Scrofula's girl, "truly bilious."

"Truly bilious?" said Nat. "Is that your name?"

The girl burst into tears and left. Now there was no one sitting opposite them.

"Stop fanning the pan, you'll make it worse," said Miss Austen to Dad. "Don't you know anything?"

"Let me tell you how I slept," said Nat. "First, I had a hundred rocks digging into my bum all night. Then the yurt was so draughty I got a chill down my side, which is now nearly paralysed and I'm not even joking. Penny snores like a big fat goat. And when it rained in the night, the rain dripped straight on to my face and I had to make Penny hold a bucket up to catch it."

"For an hour," grumbled Penny quietly.

"I said we'd take turns," snapped Nat, thinking, *If you believe that, you'll believe anything*.

"And it sounds so weird out here," continued Nat. "There's no traffic, or car alarms, or people shouting rude things at each other as they come out of the Red Lion. I don't like it."

Darius just shrugged.

"AAAAHHHHH. No one panic, it's only a small fire," yelled Dad in panic, running around in circles, holding a flaming frying pan.

A few sensible kids – and Penny – ran off.

Nat was used to Dad's cookery accidents so stayed put. Darius stayed put because he liked fires. And he also liked finishing other people's breakfasts.

"So I'm giving you one last, final, ultimate chance to clear out of that chalet and let me have it," said Nat. "You know I deserve it."

"Nope."

Nat jabbed him furiously with a beany fork.

"I'll get you, Bagley," she said.

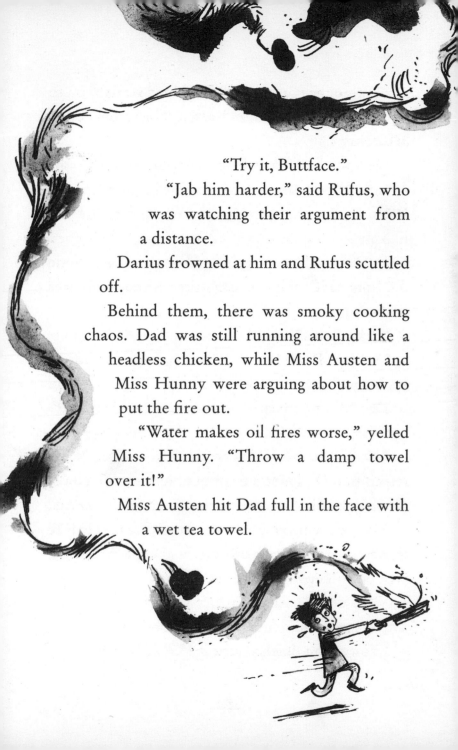

"Try it, Buttface."

"Jab him harder," said Rufus, who was watching their argument from a distance.

Darius frowned at him and Rufus scuttled off.

Behind them, there was smoky cooking chaos. Dad was still running around like a headless chicken, while Miss Austen and Miss Hunny were arguing about how to put the fire out.

"Water makes oil fires worse," yelled Miss Hunny. "Throw a damp towel over it!"

Miss Austen hit Dad full in the face with a wet tea towel.

"I meant the pan," said Miss Hunny.

"I know, I just couldn't resist hitting him," said Miss Austen.

"Don't tell Mr Dewdrop," shouted Dad, running outside. "He takes a dim view of helpers who set fire to things, even ones who are down with the kids like me."

Darius and Nat started laughing and, as she stood up, something fell out of her pocket. It glittered temptingly on the table.

"What's that?" said Darius, as Nat snatched it up.

"It's gold," she said craftily, "and you can have it if you give me your cabin."

Darius examined it. "Pyrite," he said. "It's rubbish."

"How do you KNOW this stuff?" shouted Nat in frustration. "It's flipping impossible. First off, you're a massive chimp at the bottom of the class. And anyway, you spend all your time sitting OUTSIDE the class or hanging upside down in cupboards. And I've been to your house and I know your brother Oswald doesn't have a secret collection of books. Or even *a* book."

"You gonna finish your egg?" said Darius.

Nat swiftly grabbed the egg and put it neatly down the back of his shirt. Then squished it in, for good measure.

Outside, she saw Rufus hanging around, as if he was waiting for her.

She was about to tell him to get lost, and exactly where he could put his snooty school, but he just smiled shyly at her and said, "I don't know why you're friends with IT."

Before she could think of what to say, Darius shuffled out behind her, licking bits of squished egg off his fingers.

Rufus scarpered.

Darius burped the alphabet in her ear as they headed for the eco classrooms.

Gross, thought Nat. *I bet Rufus doesn't do that.*

The children were led to a big classroom and told how the week would go.

Mornings would be spent working on geography topics intended to "inspire the project leaders to come up with their project".

That's me, thought Nat glumly, feeling less than inspired. Pretty uninspired, to be honest.

In the afternoons they would do "fun, exciting and 'bonding' camp activities".

And somewhere in all this excitement, Nat was supposed to put together a big project to show the whole flipping town just how brilliant her school was.

So this week is rank, thought Nat.

Mr Keane was giving the first lesson. He looked even more miserable than usual. He was dark-eyed and unshaven, his tie was stained with bean juice and was hanging off his neck like a limp rag, and he'd put his suit jacket on inside out. He shook a little as he faced his large class.

Outside, a crow squawked and Mr Keane jumped like he'd been shot.

"The great outdoors makes me nervous," said the geography teacher, taking a swig from a flask. "Plus I'm allergic to grass, nettles, bees, feathers, horses, wheat, flowers, soil and the common toad."

"I hope that's only tea in there, Mr Keane," said Miss Austen sternly, "and nothing stronger."

Mr Keane then had a sneezing fit, spraying the first two rows of kids.

"Can you spell 'unprofessional'?" sniggered Dr

Nobel to Miss Slippy, standing at the side of the class.

"You can, but he can't!" said Miss Austen, which Nat thought was pretty disloyal.

Mr Bungee wandered in and asked if he could watch.

"Looking forward to learning something," he said.

Nat was suspicious that he'd just come for a good laugh.

Eventually Mr Keane recovered himself and began his talk.

"Do you know that things that are long buried beneath our feet are really interesting?" he said, trying to sound positive. "So who can name something super cool you find underground?"

"Goblins," shouted Darius.

"No. Something real."

"Corpses," said Darius.

"No. Well, yes, but no—"

"The London Underground."

"Shut up, Darius," said Mr Keane. "Nathalia."

"I can't think of anything. Especially and definitely not gold," said Nat, still irritated she hadn't been able to fool Darius.

Mr Keane shook his head. "Somebody sensible. Penny?"

"Sensible?" joked Nat.

Penny looked hurt. "Atlantis?" she said eventually.

"Give me strength," said Mr Keane. "You, Marcus Milligan."

"Er, bananas?" said Marcus.

"Where do you FIND these children?" said Dr Nobel, not very quietly.

"I blame the teachers," said Miss Slippy.

"Well said," said Dad.

Miss Hunny shot him a dark look.

"Not you, Dolores," said Dad. "But the rest of them are pretty hopeless."

Everyone laughed.

Except Nat, who cringed.

And Misses Eyre and Austen, who shot Dad a look of pure hatred.

"FOSSILS!" shouted Mr Keane. "The most exciting thing in the ground ever is fossils."

With effort, he drew himself up to his full height. He was taller than he usually looked.

"AND I HAVE ONE! Who wants to see?" he said.

There was a ripple of excitement.

"Is it a T. rex skull?" said Nat.

"Or a stegosaurus plate?" said Julia Pryde, who liked using big words.

"Or even an archaeopteryx feather?" said Plum, who knew bigger ones.

Mr Keane looked faintly embarrassed. He placed something on the desk in front of him. It was a grey stone with something lumpy in it.

"It's an ammonite. A sort of seashell."

There was a moment's silence. Then everyone started laughing at him.

"You're all so mean," Mr Keane said. "Stop laughing at my tiny fossil."

"A seashell?" sneered Mr Bungee, leaning against a back wall and picking his teeth with what looked like a miniature dagger. "I hate to tell you this, mate, but there's bucketloads of shells on the beach!"

"He's SO funny," simpered Miss Austen to Miss Eyre, "and most men with muscles that big aren't."

"Is that the best fossil you've got?" said Mr Bungee.

Dr Nobel puffed himself up. "At St Scrofula's we've got the head of a velociraptor."

"Yeah, well, you've got the head of a baboon's bum. Your face," said Darius.

Five seconds later, Darius was awarded his first detention of the week.

Mr Keane was looking even more unhappy as he played with his rubbish little fossil. Nat felt embarrassed for him.

"I found this myself," muttered Mr Keane. "I thought you'd like it."

"It's not very inspiring," said Miss Slippy, sounding irritated. "How can you get the children interested in learning if you don't inspire them?"

"She's got a point," said Dad, who was talking to Mr Dewdrop. "That's why I put 'inspiring kids' first on the big long list of my great qualities."

"Whose side are you on, Ivor?" snapped Miss Hunny.

Nat put her head in her hands.

"It took me a week to find it," Mr Keane continued pathetically. "I was only twelve. I was on holiday with my mum and she thought it was brilliant. She wrote to the local paper and everything."

More howls of laughter.

Nat wanted to shout, "*SHUT UP, YOU UTTER SPANNER. YOU'RE MAKING IT WORSE.*"

"He makes our school look even more rubbish than it is," Nat said to Penny, who was too busy drawing a picture of Atlantis on the desk to even notice.

After a while, the children stopped making fun of Mr Keane long enough for him to carry on.

"I'm actually glad you think this is a useless fossil," he said in a not very convincing tone, "because I thought this week you might try to dig up a better one, right here. Lower Snotley – I mean, Lower Totley – is TEEMING with fossils. Anyone fancy that?"

No one fancied that.

He droned on for ages about Precambrian Age this and post-Jurassic Period that, and no one paid any attention. The kids started talking amongst themselves, louder and louder, until Mr Bungee pushed Mr Keane out of the way and slammed a meaty fist on the desk.

The noise shut everyone up.

"Listen up, kids!" he said. "Lemme tell you about fossils."

The children stopped chatting and listened up.

Mr Bungee held up the thing that looked like a dagger that he'd had hanging round his neck. "This," he said, "is a fossilised tooth. It's seventy million years old but it could still rip your face off."

Now the kids were very interested indeed.

"I found this tooth five years ago, high up on the cliffs by the beach. I had to hang upside down while a mate held my toes. I chipped it out of the rock face with an axe I made myself from the bones of another fossil. They reckon it's from a brand-new dinosaur. They're calling it the Bungee-saurus."

He paused. Everyone hung off his every word.

"Anyone finding a new dinosaur fossil gets to name the dinosaur," he explained. "How great is that?"

"Can we look for a fossil this week?" said Marcus Milligan.

"Sure you can," said Mr Bungee smugly.

A ripple of excitement went through the children as they huddled together.

"There you go, mate," said Mr Bungee to Mr Keane. "They're all yours."

"That's what I was trying to say," complained Mr

Keane, "but no one was listening to me."

"THAT's how you inspire kids," said Dad, "and that's how I do it too."

He took Mr Keane to one side. "It's OK," Dad said kindly, but rather too loudly for Nat's liking, "you just need more stage presence."

Nat shuddered.

"I could teach you if you like," continued Dad. "I'm a bit of an entertainer. Kids love me."

A paper aeroplane whizzed through the air and got stuck in his ear.

"Ow, that's right in my eardrum," said Dad, hopping about and making a total spectacle of himself.

Nat started sliding under the desk.

"I'm interacting with the kids," Dad added to Mr Dewdrop. "I'm totally down with them. I like their banging tunes too."

"Your dad always makes me laugh. You're so lucky to have him around to cheer you up all the time," said a gentle voice in Nat's ear.

It had the musical quality of silver bells tinkling or water bubbling over rocks. Flora Marling was SITTING NEXT TO HER!

"Blurble," said Nat.

"You're so right." Flora smiled. "Gosh, I bet one of those St Scrofula's kids finds a new fossil. They'll be on the TV news and everything. Can you imagine how HIDEOUS they'll be afterwards?"

"Flurble," said Nat.

"Yes, I agree," said Flora, "it *would* be nice if we found one first. We just need to work together and focus."

"I've drawn Atlantis," said Penny.

"Wanna hear me burp the national anthem?" said Darius, popping up from under the desk.

"Wurble," said Nat.

"Always nice talking to you," said Flora, floating off.

Nat looked around the classroom. The St Scrofula's teachers and kids were already drawing up ideas for their project, as if it was a military campaign. She saw Mr Bungee take a look at their notes and whisper something in their ears. Was he HELPING THEM?

He saw her looking and moved away.

Ooh, caught you, she thought.

Everyone from *her* school – including the teachers

– was wandering about, chatting and looking utterly gormless.

She saw Dad hovering, torn between the two schools. She knew what he was thinking. He was thinking his little girl should be sitting with the super-shiny, super-keen kids, not the ORDINARY kids.

But if I ended up at St Scrofula's it would be ACTUALLY PROPERLY IMPOSSIBLE to make friends, thought Nat. *Unless I do something, I'm in BIG trouble.*

CHAPTER TEN

• • • •

THE TWO SCHOOLS SPENT THE REST OF THE morning working on their projects.

Both schools started with the fossil idea. From what Nat could see, the swotty St Scrofula's project would include aerial photos, writing a computer program, gathering soil samples and online research. It was all on PowerPoint.

After three hours, the 8H Let's Find a Fossil Project was a big bit of paper with three words on it:

Buy spades.

Dig.

We need a better project, Nat realised. *And soooon.*

"What have you lot done?" Nat asked Plum, as

they left the classroom.

Plum looked at her as if she was an insect making an unscheduled appearance in her bowl of breakfast cereal.

"I'd love to share, but we are in a competition," Plum said, "and I'm not asking what you've done."

"Thanks," said Nat.

"You're welcome," said Plum, smirking.

After a ghastly lunch of fish-paste sandwiches and healthy snack bars that tasted of dust, both classes were herded into minibuses and driven deep into a nearby forest for today's outdoor activity: Mr Bungee's Survival Skills Class.

In the forest, iron-grey clouds hung above them, heavy with rain. A light drizzle fell.

Everyone assembled around Mr Bungee, but Nat saw Mr Keane, still sitting in their minibus, miserable and alone. He was writing something in the grime on the windows. It read:

ƎℲI⅃ YM ƎTAH I

It took her a minute to work out it was written backwards.

"Team leaders, gather round, let's do-o-oooh it!"

yelled Mr B.

"That's you, team leader moron," hissed Nat to Darius, as Rufus walked over to the big New Zealander.

Darius wasn't paying attention; he was too busy inscribing a picture in the grass with a sharp stick.

"Finish it off for me," he said, handing Nat the stick and walking off.

Nat squinted at the picture. She couldn't work out what it was at first.

Then she realised.

Ew.

"NATHALIA BUMOLÉ, WHAT ARE YOU DOING?" screeched Miss Austen, grabbing the stick off her and pointing at the drawing. "You revolting child. Scrub it out, and you can be on washing-up duty for the next two nights. Perhaps all that soapy water will wash out your dirty little mind."

I'm SO gonna get you, thought Nat, watching Darius trot over to join the other leaders.

"What are YOU doing?" said Mr Bungee, as Dad joined them.

"I'm a natural-born leader," said Dad cheerfully,

"so I assumed you'd want me." Dad smiled at Mr Dewdrop, who was writing on the clipboard.

"Go away," said shiny-headed Dr Nobel. "You'll give your school an unfair advantage."

"I think he's more of a handicap," sniggered Miss Eyre.

Nat flushed red.

"Why is everything a competition?" said Dad. "Isn't it better if we work together?"

"NO!" yelled Mr Bungee. "What's the matter? Don't like a bit of competition, eh?"

"Do your best," said Dad to Darius. "You'll probably lose, but remember: it's only a bit of fun."

"Yeah, said the losers," mocked Mr Bungee.

Nat's heart sank. Dad had already written her school off. This was terrible.

Well, she thought, *we'll see about that. We've got to start winning.*

"Right," said the big man, "let's see if any of you could survive in the wilderness."

"It's not really the wilderness though, it it?" said Dad, who was still a bit annoyed at not being recognised as a born leader. "It's more like a big park. I mean, there's a nice pub half a mile away.

Actually, I've heard they do nice steak and kidney pudding."

"Shut up about steak and kidney pudding," shouted Mr Bungee, which was pretty much what Nat was about to say. "I'm gonna teach you how to survive when the nearest pub is a thousand kilometres away."

"I wouldn't want to go anywhere that's a thousand kilometres away from a nice steak and kidney pudding," said Dad, and the kids laughed.

"Don't laugh," said Nat, "you'll only encourage him."

Mr Bungee gave Dad a filthy look. "Stop interrupting," he said. "Now, kids, survival is about quick thinking. I've got some useful equipment in my truck and I'm giving the team leaders one minute to get any items which they think might be needed in the wild."

"Now, that's clever," said Dad loudly to Mr Dewdrop. "Although it's a bit like that film and *I* like to be more original when I work with kids. I find they like it more."

Mr D wrote something on his clipboard. Dad gave Nat a quick thumbs up to show how well he thought he was doing.

Nat looked for a hedge to crawl under.

"GO!" screamed Mr Bungee.

Darius and Rufus ran to the truck, with everyone yelling encouragement.

Except Nat, who yelled annoyance at Miss Hunny.

"Miss, why did you make Darius our team leader? He's a total chimp."

"I think making him a leader is good for him," she said. "And you must keep supporting him, Nathalia – it's very important. I've been watching you recently and it's almost like you're cross with him."

Nat kicked at the ground in frustration.

After a minute, Mr B blew a whistle and the leaders showed him their wilderness survival equipment.

Rufus had a handsaw, some rope, and a fishing rod.

Darius had a packet of mints.

"Interesting," said Miss Hunny.

"Hey, that's MY packet of mints," said Mr Bungee. "They're not even part of the survival test."

"What did you get *those* for?" shouted Nat.

"I like mints," said Darius, through a mouthful of mints.

The St Scrofula's kids and teachers laughed.

Nat felt sick. They were going to do SO BADLY.

She looked at Dad, who was chatting to Dr Nobel.

"Let's play... Survivor School!" shouted Mr Bungee.

The St Scrofula's kids growled like tigers.

Nat looked at her classmates and teachers, pottering about like wombats.

We don't look like survivors, she thought. *We look like LUNCH.*

"You've got one hour," yelled Mr Bungee happily. "And I want to see each school build a fire, make a camp, and set a trap for something furry."

"Furry? Ooh, are we getting a camp pet?" said Penny, who had three cats, six hamsters, a roomful of gerbils, and a dog called Bilbo.

"Don't talk rot," drawled the Kiwi camp leader, over howls of laughter from the St Scrofula's pupils. "But if you do catch something, I'll teach you how to skin it. With your bare hands."

Penny went pale.

"Everyone, follow me," said Dad, who had

obviously decided it was time for him to take charge of the rabble. "We can start with the camp – I've seen a great place to make it in the woods. Quickly now."

No one followed as Dad jogged towards the trees. No one else moved. It seemed to take him AGES to realise he was on his own. Finally, he turned round.

"Oh, come on," he shouted, "you can trust me. I was a Boy Scout, you know."

"Shuddup, Dad, no one cares," shouted Nat. "Go and sit in the minibus."

"But I was great in the Scouts," continued Dad. "I got badges and everything. Who wants to see my badges?" He walked back towards the kids, winking at Mr Dewdrop.

Nat knew what badges Dad had won and she didn't want anyone else to find out. "We should just believe him. Let's go," she shouted.

"No, no, obviously everyone wants to see them. I brought the badges all this way because I knew they'd come in handy," said Dad, rummaging about in a rucksack and bringing out a handful of tatty old cloth badges.

He held them up, one at a time.

"This is my cooking badge," he said.

"What, like skinning and eating little bunnies?" said Penny.

The boys looked impressed.

"No, for making cupcakes," said Dad, "but I had to make them outside, of course. In the back garden, yes, but that's still outside, no matter what the other boys said."

Nat looked for a hedge to hide in.

"Plus, they had pictures of wild animals on, all drawn in icing," continued Dad. "I got extra marks for that. Although I didn't get top marks because David Spudulike ate my lion's head, the little monster."

He showed them another badge. "This is for knitting," he said.

"Knitting?" said Julia Pryde. "Are you joking?"

"It's a very important skill," said Dad, ignoring the giggles from the children. "You can make fishing nets, or bags to carry berries and nuts around in the forest. You can make a handy sweater in case it gets cold and, of course, you can always knit the word 'help'."

Help, thought Nat. *Help meeeee.*

"Although, to be fair, knitting is only really a sensible option if you're in an area with lots of sheep in," continued Dad.

Please shut up, thought Nat.

But Dad, with an audience, was now unstoppable. Worse, Nat knew they were wasting time, as she watched kids from the rival school disappear into the woods.

"This badge is for flower-pressing," said Dad, to howls of laughter. "No, listen! You might laugh, but spotting an edible marigold could save your life one day."

The howls got louder.

"This is a goodie. It's my morris-dancing one. I admit it's not much use helping you survive, but a good morris dance keeps everyone's spirits up."

Some of the children started dancing around, hitting each other with sticks, like mini morris dancers.

"You're very much *not* helping," yelled Nat, ducking as a stray stick whizzed past her left ear.

"And let's not forget my home-decorating badge."

"Which Scout troop were you in, EXACTLY?"

said Miss Austen. "Are you sure it wasn't the Brownies?"

"It wasn't an ordinary Scout troop," admitted Dad. "It was more of a breakaway group. I have to be honest: it was my Auntie Sharon's breakaway group."

"Auntie Sharon?" said Miss Eyre. "What are you talking about, man?"

Dad shuffled his feet. "I didn't want to say anything in case you thought I only got so many awards cos I was a suck-up favourite. I really earned those badges, you know."

"That's enough badges for one day," shouted Nat, thinking enough was enough. She grabbed Dad and started dragging him away. "Let's get on with this."

"I haven't shown them my other badges," said Dad, as she led him towards the woods.

"And I've got a silver cup for winning Auntie Sharon's Who Can Stay Out in the Garden the Longest Competition." Dad dropped his voice. "Although I'm not sure it counts properly because I spent an hour inside, in the kitchen at midnight getting some milk and biscuits and refilling my hot-water bottle. I think Auntie Susan saw me, but she never told."

"That's great, Dad, you've FULLY shown me up now. I'm going to build a shelter by myself where no one will EVER FIND ME."

CHAPTER ELEVEN

· · · ·

TRYING TO BUILD A CAMP WAS A TOTAL NIGHTMARE. Dad kept taking charge, which made everything way worse. After what seemed like an eternity of struggling, the children, aided by Miss Hunny (but not lazy Misses Eyre and Austen), had just about got some leafy, wet branches folded over to make a nice tent, when Dad said:

"It needs to be at a different angle. Leave it to me."

Then he charged in, shoved things around, and the whole lot fell on top of him.

"Aaaagh, I've got a leaf in my eye," he yelled from somewhere under the pile. His arms and legs stuck out, thrashing about like an upturned, leafy beetle.

Nat and Darius watched him flail about for a while. They were sitting on a slope nearby, finishing the mints.

"Thinking about it, I'm quite glad you got these," said Nat. "I mean, if you'd chosen the saw, Dad would've lost a body part by now."

"You're the leader," said Flora Marling, coming up to Darius and dropping a pile of wet logs on his head with a *clonk*, "so make the fire. I'm going to do the other part – the furry animal traps." She floated away.

I can believe in fairies when I see you, thought Nat, watching Flora in awe.

Darius coughed up a woodlouse, stared at it wiggling in his palm, then ate it.

Hmm, and I can believe in goblins too, she thought.

Darius picked a tiny leg out of his teeth and looked at the wood with an expert eye.

The logs were green and sodden, but Nat knew that if anyone could set them ablaze, it was him. She shuffled away nervously. Just in case.

"Any ideas?" she said.

Darius spat on the wood.

"That won't help," she said.

Her friend kicked the logs away and stood up.

"Can't set fire to them," he said.

"I bet you can," said Nat. "You've set fire to the chemistry lab every week all term."

"Follow me," he said, walking deep into the woods.

He didn't bother to look back to see if she was actually following, which made her irritated enough to ALMOST not follow him.

But she did; she told herself she needed to be around to keep him out of trouble. Truth was, she secretly quite liked watching the trouble.

"Where are we going?" she said, after several minutes of trekking through the woods.

"To see what the other school are doing. Sssh," he said, "you'll never be a ninja like me if you keep jabbering."

"Darius Bagley, you are not a ninja," said Nat crossly.

"I'm more of a ninja than you are," he said.

"More of a chimp," she muttered.

Then Darius jabbed a grubby finger towards a

red flickering light ahead. "Sssh, look…"

"How did they get a fire lit?" said Nat, as they watched the St Scrofula's kids and their flipping perfect camp.

They had already built a large shelter, which had even got a proper roof and chimney. In front of the building blazed a small but cheerful fire. Some of the kids had branches in their hair and mud on their faces. They looked like savages.

"They cheated," said Darius simply.

Nat peered harder. He was right! Mr Bungee was helping put the final touches to the shelter. She saw him laughing with Dr Nobel.

"Why's he helping them?" said Nat.

Darius shrugged. He studied the scene a little while longer.

Eventually he said, "I'm taking their fire. You distract them and I'll grab a burning branch."

"I don't like the sound of any of that," said Nat.

But Darius was already heading towards the camp. "Thought you didn't want them to be better than us," he said quietly.

That did it. Nat took off with a determined look on her face.

I wonder, she thought, as she got nearer, keeping out of sight, *I wonder if I should make a noise like a furry animal? Then they'd leave the camp and... Oh yeah, hunt me down with sharp sticks. That's a rubbish idea.*

Well, she decided, *if I don't want them to hunt me, I need to sound like I'm hunting THEM. I just need to sound really scary.*

She was very pleased with her logic, but as she looked at the St Scrofula's kids through a gap in the trees, she didn't think they looked very easy to scare.

She cleared her throat and wondered what kind of animal might frighten them off. The only thing she could think of was Darius, and he was busy.

In the end, she decided some low growling and a bit of bush-shaking was her best bet.

"*RRRRR*," she began, feeling like a total spanner.

No one in the camp heard her.

She shook the bush harder.

"*GRRRRRR!*" she yelled. "*GRRR, ROAR, WOOF!*"

A few of the children at the camp looked round, alarmed.

It was working!

Now Nat was having fun. She began to howl like a wolf. Surely *everyone* was scared of wolves.

"*AAAA-OOOOH!*" she began. "*HOWOO OOOL!*"

"What on Earth are you doing?" said Plum.

Who was standing RIGHT NEXT TO HER.

In her efforts not to be seen, Nat had totally failed to notice the other gir, who was in the bushes collecting berries.

"Glark," said Nat, totally caught out.

She wanted to run away, but to her horror found she was unable to move. She was rooted to the spot in utter embarrassment.

"Hey, everyone," laughed Plum, "guess who I've found spying on us? It's Bumole."

"It's pronounced Bew-mow-lay," said Nat, deciding she could move after all and kicking her hard on the shins.

"Ow, you little beast," shouted Plum, and made a grab for her.

Nat dodged easily. Being Darius's friend meant she had the reflexes of a cat in a room entirely filled with mice and balls of string.

"Everyone, let's capture her!" shouted the bruised

girl, as Nat took to her heels and fled.

She heard a great shout from the camp behind her. She crashed frantically through brambles, hopped over logs and dodged the tree trunks looming up at her.

Nat was a fast and nimble runner with her old friend BLIND PANIC on her side. She was getting away!

Right up until the moment she stepped on a trap.

Clunk, went the rope noose around her foot.

BOOIINNNG, went the bent tree, which was attached to the noose.

WHIZZ, went Nat, yanked upside down through the air.

"WAAAAH!" yelled Nat, dangling like a

fish on a rod.

"Well done," said Darius, running underneath her with a burning branch. "What a great distraction. I managed to pinch a branch AND put their fire out. Good job I had that extra can of pop today." He ran right past her.

"Get me down, you horror," yelled Nat.

"No time to hang around." Darius grinned, disappearing. "See you later."

CHAPTER TWELVE

• • • •

NAT WAS FOUND, A MINUTE LATER, BY MR BUNGEE, who put his meaty hands on his hips and laughed like a drain. The other children joined him, and Nat, swinging gently in the breeze, had to endure an eternity of mocking laughter before Dr Nobel and Miss Slippy bent the branch down and set her free.

"Well, we caught a big one," roared Mr Bungee, "although there's not much meat on her."

Dazed and humiliated, Nat bared her teeth and produced the sort of noise that she'd been trying to make earlier. Only this time, she was genuinely, properly scary. Her long blonde hair flew around her face like a cavewoman who'd stopped making an effort and decided to let herself go.

Nat advanced on her tormentors like a real wild animal. Which, basically, she was.

"You're all gonna get it," she hissed, grabbing a large heavy stick from the ground and swinging it like a club. Nat was handy with a rounders bat; she had lost more balls over the roof of the housing estate opposite the playing fields than anyone.

Everyone took a step back. They all looked nervous – except Rufus, who had a strange look on his face Nat didn't recognise.

"Now now, young lady, you're all right. There's no harm done," said Miss Slippy, moving towards the furious girl.

"Who set that trap?" said Nat. "Cos they're first. I'm having all of you, but they're first."

"Where on Earth do these children come from?" said Plum nervously. "I don't think we should be mixing with them."

The other children seemed to agree, because they'd already run off.

"Wait for me," Plum yelled, following.

Nat faced the teachers, still holding her stick.

"Put down the stick," said Dr Nobel. "You've made your point, now don't do anything you'll regret."

"I won't," said Nat. "I really won't regret it."

As he advanced, Dr Nobel's large, shiny, bald head swam into Nat's view. A reddish mist had drifted across her eyes, and now his head looked like A MASSIVE ROUNDERS BALL.

She drew her arm back as far as she could, shifting her weight to get in her best rounders batting position and…

…someone snatched the stick from her hand, just as she let fly.

Without the stick, Nat whirled around twice before flopping dizzily to the ground.

Behind her, Dad was saying, "I'll take her back now. I'll make her a nice cuppa. Brewed on our lovely, warm fire." He scooped Nat up off the ground and carted her off.

By the time they got back to their makeshift camp, Nat had recovered from her rage.

"I think all the blood ran to my head while I was hanging there," she explained, as Dad put her down. "I turned into Oswald Bagley for a minute."

Dad shuddered at the name. Oswald was Darius's mad, bad, and beardy older brother, the terror of the town. Unfortunately for Darius, Oswald looked after him.

"I thought Oswald might be better now he's married," said Dad. "Turns out he just made his wife worse."

Darius was sitting by the fire, toasting worms.

"Do NOT tell anyone what just happened," she growled.

"OMG, Nat," said Penny, sitting next to her. "Are you OK? Darius told me all about it."

Nat glared at him.

He grinned.

"It's OK cos I was sworn to secrecy," added Penny. "I only told one other person."

Just then, everyone in the camp started pointing at Nat and laughing.

"Oh, can no one keep a secret?" said Penny.

"I always said she was highly strung," chuckled Julia Pryde, looking at Nat.

"Hilarious," said Nat.

"You trying to get above yourself?" said Milly Barnacle.

"Good one," said Nat. "Any more, people? Let's have them."

Nat had learned a long time ago that the best way to stop people laughing behind her back was to let them do it to her front. It was painful but over quicker, like an aching tooth being yanked out, or a plaster coming off a scab.

Finally, everyone ran out of jokes and Nat went to help continue building the shelter.

Dad had been doing his best, which meant it was rubbish, but at least he hadn't nailed himself to anything or blown it up. Which was what usually happened when Dad did DIY.

Still, Nat had to admit it wasn't very good. It was all wonky and there were great big holes in it. She wouldn't have wanted the Dog to sleep in it.

"Call this a hut?" said a familiar voice. It was Mr Bungee, and he was marking their school's efforts.

"What's wrong with it?" said Dad, who was on tiptoes, struggling to put a branch on the roof.

"One gust of wind and it'll tip right over," said Mr Bungee.

"Rubbish," said Dad, turning round quickly and losing his balance. "Oh heck," he said, and fell straight into the hut, which collapsed around him.

"Now, how about your traps?" said Mr Bungee. "Did you build any?"

"No one wanted to catch furry animals but we did dig up some worms," said Miss Hunny.

"Worms? You can't eat those," said Mr Bungee.

"Wrong," burped Darius in Nat's ear, sucking on his stick.

"And your fire…" said the big New Zealander, moving over to Nat and Darius.

"It's a good fire," said Nat.

"Yeah, it is. Problem being, your fire was stolen from the other school."

"But you were helping the other team!" said Nat, jumping to her feet in outrage. "I saw you."

"No one's gonna believe what YOU saw," he laughed, taking her swiftly to one side. "You're the girl who couldn't see a great big noose on the ground."

Because Nat's class was judged to be the worst at survival skills, they had to wash up after dinner. Again. They were all tired and irritable, and small scuffles broke out every now and again.

"Marcus Milligan, are you holding Peaches

Bleary's head under the soapy water again?" said Miss Hunny, yet again. "Please stop it. You're showing us all up."

"Shall I organise a singalong tonight?" said Dad cheerfully.

Everyone groaned.

"I'll take that as a yes," he said. "Now, if I can just find my ukulele…"

"What's this at the bottom of the sink?" said Penny, dredging up a ukulele. "It looks like a guitar that's been shrunk in the hot water."

"Shush," said Nat, pushing the ukulele back under the bubbles, "the day's been horrible enough."

"You're using far too much washing-up liquid," complained Miss Slippy, who was sticking her nose in where it wasn't wanted.

Nat's arms were covered in bubbles. She looked like a half-melted snowman.

"Our science lab helped create this," said Dr Nobel smugly, holding up a tub of thick washing-up gloop. "It's totally safe and biofriendly AND it still bubbles better than the other leading brands."

Are you a teacher or a salesman? thought Nat grumpily.

Dad, of course, was terribly impressed. He peered at the label.

"Look at this, Nat. Super-duper Eco-Earth Hug-the-world washing-up liquid."

"So what?"

Dr Nobel looked even smugger than usual, which wasn't easy but he managed it. "It was in all the papers," he said. "You know, the big papers, so you might not have noticed. The real newspapers, not the ones that just have pictures of footballers falling out of cars after a party."

"Yes, I know the ones you mean," said Dad, who read the ones with pictures of footballers in.

"We won a big cash prize. It's given us the money to buy a new science block."

"Wow," said Dad, "your school is so amazing."

Urgh, Dad the fan-boy, groaned Nat to herself. *It's revolting.*

It was worrying too.

"Oi," she interrupted, splashing the bubbles around, "we're getting a new science block too, so there."

"Hmm," said Miss Hunny, walking past, "but that's only because of the insurance money we got after Darius blew it up."

"He didn't blow ALL of it up, Miss," said Nat quickly, "and it was really old and smelly anyway. The Head said he did us a favour. She'd been thinking of doing it herself, Mr Keane told me. He volunteered to do it himself, actually."

"Where DO you send your daughter to school?" said Dr Nobel to Dad.

"Actually, can I talk to you about that?" said Dad, sending a chill through Nat.

The two of them walked off, chatting. Nat was HORRIFIED.

She wanted to follow and do some sneaky spying, but mean Miss Slippy said she'd have to stay and do the drying too.

She plunged her hands into the soapy water in fury. She just KNEW what Dad was talking about.

But what could she do about it?

"OW!" she yelled, as Penny turned the taps on full, almost scalding her with hot water. "Penny, you spanner, that's *nuclear* hot!"

And then she had an idea.

CHAPTER THIRTEEN

••••

"I'M GOING NUCLEAR," SAID NAT.

Penny snapped wide awake. They were in their sleeping bags. It was the dead of night. A barn owl hooted somewhere and a small, over-adventurous mouse found himself whisked off his feet and wished he hadn't gone into the deep, dark, owl-filled wood.

"Not...?" said Penny, suddenly understanding. "You can't mean...?"

"I can mean and I do mean."

"No, Nat, it's too dangerous. He's like a doomsday weapon, anything might happen. We might get blowback."

"Don't care. It's the only way," said Nat. "I'm

setting off… DARIUS."

There was a horrid, deep silence. Both girls knew it could end horribly.

"If WE can't WIN at anything – and, let's be honest, we can't – then THAT SCHOOL HAS TO LOSE. I don't know how, but if anyone can ruin their lives, it's Darius."

"But you've been arguing with him since we got here," said Penny. "Will he do it for you?" She spoke in a hushed tone.

"Don't worry, I'll ask him nicely," said Nat.

"Get lost. You can't have my cabin. Go away," said Darius, early the next morning.

He was still in his sleeping bag and Nat had just kicked the cabin door open.

She started shouting at him as pale morning sunlight crept in through the open door and fell on his pasty face.

"Aaargh, too loud and too much light," he said, ducking his face into the sleeping bag.

Quick as a flash, Nat zipped the top up completely and sat on him as he wriggled about like a fat green maggot.

"Gerroff, it smells in here," said Darius, trapped and muffled.

"I know, that's why I'm keeping the stink in," said Nat. "Now listen, I need your help."

"And this is definitely the best way to get it," said squished Darius.

That just annoyed Nat. She jumped up and down on him.

"Too much stomping," said Darius.

"WILL…"

STOMP.

"…YOU…"

STOMP.

"…DO…"

STOMP.

"…IT?"

"YES, I'LL DO IT," said Darius eventually. "Do what?"

"You have to make that stuck-up school look even worse than ours so my dad doesn't make me go there."

Darius just laughed.

"Don't be mad," he said eventually.

"You're an evil doom genius," she argued.

"Yeah, but I'm not Voldemort."

"Meaning?"

"It's impossible. Have you seen them? They're perfect. I heard their *caretaker's* got ten GCSEs."

"Oh heck. Our caretaker's got a pet goat and a spider-web tattoo on his neck."

"Right. So it can't be done. Go away now, I'm sleepy."

"Do something sneaky and evil to them, I don't care what," said Nat, shaking him. "Otherwise they're going to make us look like the worst school ever on Saturday, in front of everybody, when they win the competition."

"And?" said Darius.

"AND it'll be me up there getting laughed at. AND my daft dad thinks they're brilliant already and that'll be the final straw and the next thing you know I'll be sent there. AND you'll be left with no friends."

Darius looked at her big, stompy, friendly footmarks all over his sleeping bag.

"Stop looking at those," said Nat.

"Why are you always so worried about friends?" asked Darius. "What's the big deal?"

"You don't understand because you're a – well, I'm not quite sure WHAT you are – but for normal people friends are THE MOST IMPORTANT THING."

"So why are you so rubbish at them then?" said Darius.

"I'm working with poor-quality materials," snapped Nat. "Meaning 8H. Oh, come on, chimpy, help me out. Plus you like being sneaky and evil."

"True," said Darius. "I do like that. OK, lemme think."

Nat stared at him.

"On my own," he said, burrowing back into his sleeping bag.

That morning, it was Dr Nobel's lesson. Nat really hoped it would be utterly rubbish and put Dad off.

But even as she walked into the classroom, she knew it was going to be AWESOME.

Pants, she thought, as she stared at a huge model of A VOLCANO.

It was over a metre high, a huge grey-brown cone that looked like it was made from solid rock. It was a perfect scale model; it even had a few tiny trees dotted around the base. And, best of all, there was even a wisp of smoke coming from the top!

All the kids were impressed.

"Careful," said Dr Nobel, as they crowded around excitedly, "it's an active volcano!"

"Aren't volcanoes a bit like flowers?" said Penny. "Don't they die when you cut them down?"

"This isn't a real volcano," said Dr Nobel, "and, no, they're not like flowers. I thought you lot were all supposed to be good at geography?"

"She was only joking," said Nat hastily.

She thought fast. Too fast.

"We're a brilliant geography school really, but we're also… a centre for comedy."

"What?"

"You know," said Nat, "some schools are good at maths or science or English. We're good at jokes."

Miss Slippy whispered, "That explains her father."

"I heard that," said Nat. "Take it back. My dad is not a joke. In fact, he's never been funny in his life, ever."

"Hang on, love," said Dad, listening nearby. "I am top funny." He put his Green Bogey hat on. "I AM funny, aren't I, kids?"

They laughed.

Nat gave up and sat down.

When everyone was ready, Dr Nobel stood in front of the smoking model and said, "I heard that yesterday you looked at something old, dead, and useless – that was Mr Keane."

Everyone laughed except Nat, Darius, and Dad. And Mr Keane.

"Oh, sorry," said Dr Nobel, who wasn't sorry at all. "Slip of the tongue. What I meant was, WITH Mr Keane. I was talking about his fossil."

"But he meant Mr Keane too, that's why it's funny," explained Miss Austen to Miss Eyre.

"Anyway, today we're looking at VOLCANOES. And I'd like to thank our art teacher, Mr Painter, for lending us this model of Mount Etna, which he built for the horror film *The Volcano Monster versus Sharktopus Rex*."

"Could your school get any more amazing?" said Dad.

Nat wanted to be sick. Properly sick. *Hopefully on suck-up Dad*, she thought.

"Please, Sir, what's making it smoke?" said Rufus.

"Lava, dummy," said Penny, who wanted to make

up for her previous dumb remark – by unwisely making another dumb remark.

Everyone laughed at her. Including Nat.

"Sorry," said Nat, as Penny glared at her. "OMG, chill."

"Just a basic fogger," Darius muttered in Nat's ear. "A mixture of propane and glycol."

"It's a very clever mixture of two liquids called propane and glycol," said Dr Nobel slowly, "but you don't need to worry about that until you do your GCSE chemistry."

Nat looked at Darius. "Lucky guess," she said. "And never mind procol or glycane or whatever it is, how's the evil plan of doom going?"

Before Darius could say anything, Dr Nobel raised his voice. "If I could have EVERYONE'S attention," he said, meaning Darius and Nat, "I can begin unravelling the mysteries of the smoking mountains."

And unravel the mysteries they did. In thirty minutes Nat was forced to admit she'd already learned more than she had in a month of Mr Keane's rubbish lessons.

This is not going well, she thought, looking at

Dad's face. He was ENTRANCED.

Mr Keane just looked faintly embarrassed. *You've just been owned*, thought Nat.

Towards the end of the lesson, Dr Nobel announced, "And now... the big finish. Stand back, she's going to blow!"

There was a great rumbling from the model. Thick smoke poured out, rolling down the slope.

Then there was a horrible grinding of gears, a nasty *BOINK* sound, an apologetic cough, and the smoky mountain fell silent. And not smoky.

"Oh," said Dr Nobel, "something's gone wrong."

Ha, thought Nat, *you're not perfect after all.*

Dr Nobel peered into the cone.

"Sorry," he said, "technical hitch." He turned to the audience and said half-jokingly, "I don't suppose there are any young engineers here as well as young geographers?"

Darius walked forward. "Me," he said.

Nat was amazed. She knew Darius was a whizz with engines – he was always fixing Dad's rotten old camper van, the Atomic Dustbin. BUT HE NEVER EVER VOLUNTEERED TO HELP. EVER. What was he up to?

It didn't seem to matter because Dr Nobel didn't believe him anyway.

Dr Nobel laughed. "Be serious," he sneered.

Miss Hunny rushed over, her long cardigan sleeves flapping about like wings. She put a protective arm around the boy.

"Ooh, stop being so undermining," she said. "That's not what I call good teaching."

Dr Nobel just cleared his throat. "Hmm," he said.

"I made Darius our team leader, don't forget," she said. "I've got every faith in him, even if you haven't." She put her hand on the very top of his head; it was the safest part of him to touch because it was the least likely to be sticky.

Nat watched as Darius went a bit cross-eyed. She sighed. Darius always went funny around Miss H; she had NO IDEA why.

But Nat quite liked her form teacher – she'd have liked her a whole lot more if she hadn't been Dad's oldest friend – and she liked the fact that she always stuck up for Darius.

"All right," Dr Nobel finally agreed. "Then the volcano is all yours, young man. There's a hatch at the back where you can get into the – oh."

Darius just popped down the big hole at the top of the model.

"Will he be all right in there?" asked Dr Nobel.

"Oh yes," said Miss Hunny, "he really likes small dark spaces. It's everyone else at school that's scared of them – well, we are now that we know Darius might be lurking in one."

Dr Nobel shook his head.

"You know," said Miss Hunny, trying to make conversation as they heard banging and rude words coming from the volcano, "there's been a vacancy at our school for a new chemistry teacher ever since the, erm…" she pointed towards the volcano and Darius, "…ever since THE INCIDENT. You could do worse than apply."

"No, I couldn't do worse," said Dr Nobel. "I really couldn't."

He peeked down the hole.

"Don't surprise Darius," said Miss Hunny, dragging him away. "We've learned not to do that – he doesn't like it."

"Is it time for the Green Bogey to entertain everyone?" said Dad. "I mean, if you're having trouble finishing your lesson…"

Dr Nobel looked angry. "I don't need your help in my lesson," he said.

"It's just that your class looks distracted," said Dad helpfully.

It was true. All the kids were now chatting and laughing, except for a couple of the bigger boys who were having a quiet scrap at the back.

"This is YOUR bad influence," said Dr Nobel, surveying the chaos. "My pupils would never even *talk* in lessons, let alone – oh dear! Stop doing that, Tarquin."

He ran over to stop Tarquin doing whatever it was he needed to stop doing. But by now the St Scrofula's children were enjoying this new fun thing they'd just discovered – MESSING ABOUT IN CLASS.

Dr Nobel looked thoroughly confused. His perfect lesson was falling apart at the seams.

He hurried back to the volcano and shouted down the cone, "You can come out now. You've caused enough trouble."

But Darius wasn't going anywhere.

"Get lost. I've always wanted to live in a volcano," he said.

"He has, Sir," said Nat. "To be fair to him, he HAS always wanted to live in a volcano. He's been making plans for a lair of doom for ages, and there's always been a volcano in them."

"Is everyone at your school totally insane?" said Dr Nobel.

"Nathalia, get Darius out," said Miss Hunny. She turned to the good doctor. "And, by the way, WE'RE the normal school, not you," she said primly.

Suddenly Nat felt oddly proud of her soppy teacher.

"Do as you're told, Nathalia. Hurry, don't show me up like this," said Miss Hunny sternly.

Nat scowled and felt less proud.

Miss Hunny turned back to Dr Nobel. The noise from the restless children was growing. Little beads of sweat were bubbling on his bald head. A stressed-out red vein throbbed alarmingly.

"Nathalia has a special way with Darius," said Miss Hunny. "At our school we like to cater to pupils' needs individually. Everyone is unique to us; everyone gets special care and attention."

"GET OUT, YOU MASSIVE CHIMP, OR YOU'RE DEAD," yelled Nat down the hole. "I'll drop hot sick on you in a minute."

"Hey, guess what?" said Darius.

Nat stuck her head over the hole. "What?" she said.

"I found out how to make it do this," said Darius.

And a MASSIVE blast of oily smoke belched out of the volcano, hitting Nat square in the face.

"BLAAAARGH!" she gasped, stepping back. A horrid, sticky, black mess covered her face and hair. She blinked, revealing two white eyes. She just knew she looked like a cartoon explosion.

The whole class fell about laughing.

YET AGAIN I'M A LAUGHING STOCK, she thought. *WHY ME?*

"That's for stomping," said Darius.

BAGLEY.

That was the reason.

BAGLEY MUST DIE.

In fury, Nat dived head-first down the volcano cone. There was a quick scuffle and then Darius emerged from the hatch at the back.

"Where are you, you little monster?" yelled Nat, upside down. "I've got gunk in my eyes and I can't see a flipping thing."

Her feet were sticking out of the tip of the model. They wiggled about, as Darius took a bow to wild applause.

Nat realised what had happened but was now completely stuck upside down in the model.

"Stop messing, love," said Dad, coming over and grabbing her ankles. "I think you've distracted people enough."

Distracted? Dad always thought she ENJOYED making people laugh, just because he did. But she didn't find her life funny one little bit. Oh no. What she had learned to do was PRETEND she was trying to be funny. That way, people didn't take the mickey QUITE as much.

Dad heaved her out and wiped her face down with a clean hanky.

Nearby, Rufus was squaring up to Darius.

"You're supposed to be a friend to Nathalia but

you're a… jolly rotten one," he said.

"Come on, lads," said Mr Bungee, getting in between them, "settle down. Show's over. Everyone, let's give Dr Nobel a big hand for a great lesson, eh?"

Nat got cleaned up as best she could in the shower block. When she came out, the volcano creature himself was waiting.

"Dead man walking, Bagley," she said. "I'm gonna get you."

"That idiot Rufus likes you," said Darius.

"Doesn't," said Nat. "Shut up."

"Yes he does, and that's good – very good. We can use the enemy's strength against them."

Nat often wondered what Darius's mind looked like. It made her shudder.

He was grinning his familiar evil grin. "I've got a plan now. You have to be a double agent. First, you gotta pretend that we've fallen out."

"That's easy, dog breath, cos you won't give me the flipping cabin."

"Yes, act just like that," said Darius.

Nat fumed.

"Then," he continued, "you need to be the idiot

Rufus's friend. Get him to tell you about their project so we can get them from within."

"What? *Get them from within?* No. I'm not being sneaky and evil. *You're* the one who needs to be sneaky and evil."

"I am being sneaky and evil. You just need to do as you're told."

He walked off.

Nat stamped her foot. It wasn't fair. Darius was being bossy. And that was HER job.

CHAPTER FOURTEEN

· · · ·

A LITTLE LATER, NAT WAS SITTING IN A FIELD with Penny, telling her about the evil plan. Recovered from the volcano disaster, she was actually feeling quite smug that she'd got Darius to agree to nobble St Scrofula's; otherwise she might have been worried that the opposition were all busy working on their project, while no one from 8H was doing anything other than moaning about how unfair life was.

"You know," said Penny, "it's just a mad idea but maybe we should think about how we could make our school look *better* rather than make another school look worse."

"You're right," said Nat, and Penny smiled. "That is a mad idea."

Penny sighed.

Nat's voice trailed off as she stared for a while at the golden hair of Flora Marling, sitting chatting nearby. Flora was surrounded by her usual group of friends. Actually, Nat always thought of them as fans.

She wondered if she dared say hello…

"It's time for the Green Bogey," said Dad, walking up to Nat and interrupting her daydream. "I'll get my hat. I've had a great idea to stop you lot getting bored."

"No one wants the Green Bogey, Dad," said Nat, "and no one's bored."

"Listen for the drum," said Dad, wandering off happily.

"Tell me the sneaky evil plan again," said Penny, who was making daisy chains.

Nat sighed. "It's very complicated for you, but basically it starts by me and Darius looking like we've fallen out this week. Which is easy cos loads of people have seen us arguing already. Can you at least remember that?"

"You're so bossy," said Penny, "no wonder Darius has fallen out with you."

Nat gave up and closed her eyes. *All that plotting was tiring*, she thought. *A small nap in the sunshine…*

She was woken five minutes later by a really annoying drum nearby.

Thud thud thud.

Dad, she thought. *Always Dad. What's the big idiot up to now?*

She stomped off to find out, Penny tagging along behind. They followed the sound of the drumming and discovered the Green Bogey in the field next door.

Dad was sitting on a big tartan blanket. He was banging on a big drum and was wearing his stupid green hat and a stupid grin.

"It's the Green Bogey Story-writing Workshop," said Dad. "This drum is to summon those who want to speak the truth through a made-up story."

"Dad, you can't tell the truth through a made-up story. That's why it's called made-up," said Nat. "The truth is called the news. Even you should know that."

By now, a few children were coming out of their

yurts to see what all the banging was about.

"Dad, stoppit, people are looking at you," said Nat.

"That's the idea," said Dad. "Over here," he yelled, beckoning the children towards him. "Come and drink from the wellspring of inspiration."

"Dad, you sound like you've been drinking from that big wine box Mum brought back from the airport," said Nat. "You've gone properly weird since you came here, and I don't like it."

"I feel free out here, love," said Dad.

Nat was uncomfortably aware that he was getting a bigger and bigger audience.

"I'm thinking when we get home we should look at living more simple lives," Dad continued, "getting back to nature."

"Dad, you do this to me every time we go on holiday. When we rented that caravan in Norfolk you said you wanted to be a traveller."

"That's true," admitted Dad.

"I'd like to be a traveller," said Penny. "I'd have a white horse to pull my caravan and I'd sing songs and make people happy."

"Hear that, Dad? You're basically Penny

Posnitch. Happy now?"

"Hey," said Penny, offended.

But Nat was in full flow.

"And when we went to Spain you said you wanted to give up writing Christmas-cracker jokes and fight bulls instead."

"I still might," said Dad defensively. "Don't squash my dreams."

"And after you took me on the pedalos in Blackpool you said you wanted to sail around the world single-handed, looking for white whales."

"I was joking," fibbed Dad.

"Ooh, you massive fibber," said Nat, unaware their conversation was causing much tittering. "You always get carried away and have daft ideas that never get us anywhere. Why can't you be like other dads and just have a proper job and a shed?"

"Hello," said a voice next to her. It was Rufus.

Nat was about to tell him to get lost, when Penny nudged her and she remembered that Darius had basically said: BE NICE TO RUFUS.

Apparently it was very important, although he hadn't explained why.

So she smiled and said hello back.

Rufus went bright red and walked away.

That puzzled her but she didn't have time to think any more about it because now there were enough children gathered for Dad to start his Green Bogey Story-writing Workshop.

Nat noticed that, aside from her and Penny, the only children to turn up were from the rival school. *That's because everyone at my school knows Dad,* she thought. *He's made them suffer enough already.*

"Forget those boring English lessons," said Dad, in his ridiculous hat. "This is real writing – it's raw, it's from the heart, it's totally cool and street."

"It's not street, it's in a field," said Plum, who liked to get her facts straight.

"Field is more street than street," said Dad, "you get me?"

"How can anything be more street than an actual street?" said Plum.

Nat could see Dad was already getting flustered.

"Look, forget the street thing," he said. "That's not important."

"It seems to be important because you keep talking about it," said Plum.

"What's actually important," he said, tapping

himself on the chest, "is what's under your shirt."

"My vest?" said Penny.

"No, your heart," said Dad. "That's where the best stories come from."

"I thought they came from books," said a stern girl with sensible glasses.

"They have to get IN the books first," said Dad. "Now, does anyone know how stories get IN a book?" He spoke very slowly and looked at the kids like he was about to reveal a big secret.

"A writer gives it to their agent, who sells it to a publisher. The marketing team do the publicity and then the lawyers work out the contract details with bookshops and other point-of-sale outlets," said the serious girl with glasses.

"You're forgetting electronic publication like e-readers," said a serious boy. "It's a growing market."

"Good point, George."

"I might make some notes," said Dad. "Can you repeat all that? It was terrific."

"Dad, you're rubbish at this," said Nat, "really very poor indeed."

"Don't heckle me, I need my confidence," said

Dad. "I told Mr Dewdrop to come over. I need to look great. You two, keep a lookout for him." He turned back to the children.

Penny and Nat peeked over the hedge.

"Now, because I'm a real, proper writer, everyone asks me the same thing," he said. "Can you guess what it is?"

"How much money do you earn?" said Rufus.

"Erm, no," said Dad. "They ask me where I get my ideas for my writing."

"How much money DO you earn?" insisted Rufus. Is it millions?"

"No, silly, we've never heard of him," said Plum. "He's one of those writers who aren't any good."

"I AM good as a matter of fact," said Dad. "I'll have you know, I can get paid ten pounds for a single joke. How about that?"

"I can get that for washing my dad's car," said Rufus.

"I can get that for walking the dog," said Plum.

"There you go, Dad," said Nat. "Two new careers for you right there."

"Can we stop talking about money please?" said Dad. "It's not important to us creative people."

"That's what you say to Mum," said Nat, "and then you get shouted at."

She had meant to say it under her breath, but a few kids near her heard and laughed.

Dad looked hurt.

"Sorry," muttered Nat. "Carry on. I'll look out for Mr Dewdrop."

Dad carried on. "What I'm always asked is this: 'Where do you get your ideas from?'"

The children looked like they didn't care where he got his ideas from.

"Can I bang your drum?" said a boy with very short hair and sticky-out ears. "I only came to have a go on the drum."

"This is really important stuff I'm telling you," said Dad. "Please be interested."

Nat was almost starting to feel sorry for him. But not quite, the big idiot.

"Ideas are all around you, like pretty butterflies," said Green Bogey Dad, waving his hands about.

One girl squealed. "I hate butterflies," she said. "They sting."

"No they don't, you moron," said the big-eared, drum-loving boy.

"Don't you call me a moron, you... wretch," the girl replied.

"You're a perfidious worm," said the boy.

"And you are a craven coxcomb."

"In that case you're a puking, pox-ridden pignut."

Dad turned to Nat. "Why doesn't anyone at your school talk like this?" he said, impressed.

In the distance, Nat spotted a familiar figure trudging past the yurts, carrying a clipboard.

"Dad, hurry up and improve," she said. "He's coming! Mr Dewdrop's on his way."

It took another full minute for Dad to stop the row, but finally everyone settled down and he got his workshop back on track.

"To write a story," he said, "you take something real, something that actually happened. Then you make something up that's similar to the real thing so you can ACTUALLY talk about the thing that's *real*. Yeah? Good, huh?"

He paused to let his words of wisdom sink in.

"Then why don't you just write down the thing that's real in the first place?" said Rufus, confused. "Why bother to make it up?"

"Good question. Excellent question, top marks.

Because when you make it up you can make it funny," said Dad.

"Or make it sad," said Plum, who was one of those girls who liked sad stories, usually about handsome vampires being sad.

"I suppose so," said Dad, who hated sad things. "But funny's better. I mean, just think about your absolute favourite TV show. It's funny, right? Everyone loves funny."

Nat looked at Dad's audience. She noticed that most were girls. She knew what their favourite TV show was. It was her favourite show. It was *every* girl's favourite show at the moment. And it wasn't funny one little bit.

It was called *My Doomed Life* and it was basically all about how vampires made rubbish boyfriends.

"If you write about vampires, they're the best at being sad because they live for absolutely ages so they have loads of things to be sad about. Can you imagine how many things you can be sad about if you live for ever?" said Plum in a faraway voice.

"That's so sad," said Penny. "I hadn't thought of that." She started to sniff.

Some of the other girls joined in.

"Sad people are just so… sad," said the girl with sensible glasses.

"I'm sad thinking about sad people," said another girl.

"OMG, that's the saddest thing I've ever heard," said another.

"Jokes are good," said Dad, starting to get alarmed at the growing tide of misery.

Over the hedge, Nat could see Mr Dewdrop getting closer.

"Who knows any jokes?" said Dad.

But by now the sniffing was reaching something of a soggy climax.

"Dad, change the subject," hissed Nat.

Mr Dewdrop was nearly within earshot.

"Got it," said Dad. "Will everyone stop snivelling and listen to a magic secret."

The children looked at him.

"Is it a magic trick?" said Plum.

"It sort of is. Here it is. You can take ANY horrible thing that's happened and, with a bit of effort, make it totally hilarious," said Green Bogey Dad. "How about that?"

"My Great-auntie Dolly died last year," said

Plum. "That's not funny."

"Ah, um…" said Dad, flustered.

"What's funny about my dead Great-auntie Dolly?" said Plum.

Then something terrible happened. Nat saw it coming before anyone else. You see, Dad was one of those people who LAUGHED AT THE WRONG TIME. She didn't know why he did it. She had a feeling it was when Dad got nervous, because she'd seen him do it loads when Mum was telling him off and he *definitely* wasn't supposed to laugh. Like when he set fire to the living-room curtains with that 'relaxing' candle he bought, or ran out of petrol on the motorway, or bought an emu at an auction by mistake.

It was almost as if Dad laughed on purpose, to make things worse.

Because it ALWAYS MADE THINGS WORSE.

And laughing at Plum's late Great-auntie Dolly dying was definitely the VERY WORST THING HE COULD DO.

So it was with utter horror and a creeping sense of doom that Nat saw, around the corner of his mouth, the faintest traces of… a grin!

Oh no, she thought, *please, noooooo*.

And poor Plum was making it worse. Her great-auntie had managed to expire in a sadly HILARIOUS way.

"Great-auntie Dolly was in the loo," began Plum. "It took her ages because she wouldn't eat veg."

"Hnnng," said Dad, mouth twitching at the sides, trying to look sad. And failing horribly.

"She'd put a steamed roly-poly pudding on top of the cooker but she was in there so long it boiled dry and exploded."

"Oh dear," said Dad, shaking. "Oh my days… I'm so sad I'm doing that face which looks very similar to laughing like a hyena."

Plum, not looking up, carried on. "A big piece of hot flying roly-poly shot up the cat's bum and it ran out in the garden and got stuck in the tree. The fire brigade had to be called."

"This is a very sa— ah-ah —ad story," said Dad through gritted teeth. "So very, very, nnnnnng, sa— ha-hee-ho-ha sad."

"The firemen rescued the cat, but when they drove off they ran Great-auntie Dolly over."

That did it.

"AH, HA, HA, HA, HAAAA!" burst out Dad, who couldn't keep it in any longer.

"It isn't funny one teeny-tiny bit," yelled Plum, jumping up in fury. "Great-auntie Dolly was squished flat."

That just made it *worse*.

Dad roared. "I'm sorry," he said. "I can't help it."

Plum went bright purple, like a plum. "You're laughing at my squished great-auntie," she said. "How *could* you?"

And before Dad could stop chortling long enough to explain, they heard the furious voice of Mr Dewdrop, WHO HAD OBVIOUSLY HEARD EVERYTHING.

"MR BUMOLÉ, PLEASE STOP LAUGHING AT THAT POOR GIRL," shouted Mr Dewdrop. His voice was no longer soft and high-low, just very, very shocked and angry.

"I would, but you didn't hear the story," said Dad. "It's really funny. Does that make a difference?"

Uh-oh, thought Nat. *Dad's never going to get that certificate now.*

CHAPTER FIFTEEN

••••

"HE'S GIVEN ME A BLACK MARK, BUT BECAUSE he'd given me two gold stars this week already, I have one last chance to get my certificate," said Dad, a little while later. "So no harm done."

They were sharing one of Dad's pork pies, sitting by a neighbouring field full of grumpy cows.

"Best thing you can do is stay in your yurt for the rest of the week," said Nat, "then you can't possibly get into trouble."

"Yes, but I still need to look like I know what I'm doing."

"But you don't! You don't know anything."

"I do and I'm going to prove it. I've volunteered

to lead an outward-bound expedition to the Bleak Peak in a few days."

Outward-bound expedition? Bleak Peak? What new madness was this?

"Dad, you're not safe to lead an expedition to the *shops*. You get lost going to the bottom of our road."

"Only once, and that was because I was in a hurry."

"Lift up your left hand."

Dad lifted up his right hand.

"You're a menace, Dad. You can't do it."

"OK, look. Don't say anything to Mr Dewdrop, love," he said. "I need to impress him because I really need my certificate. And you'll just have to come with me, that's all."

"I'm not going on an expedition with you – are you mad?"

"But you're good at map-reading," said Dad patiently. "No one need ever know it's you helping. It'll be our little secret."

"Will you owe me a favour?"

"I suppose so."

"Then I'll think about it," said Nat.

Mrs Ferret came bustling up from the eco camp office.

"Mr Bumolé, there's someone on the phone for you," she said. "Something about a funeral, but the line's terrible. It sounds like they're talking with a mouth full of cake with no teeth in."

Nat and Dad looked at each other. They both knew it could only mean one thing.

BAD NEWS NAN.

Dad went off to get the phone call. He came back a few minutes later. They were right.

"Your nan's in Lower Totley and wants to take us for lunch," said Dad. "I've asked permission and we can go."

Obviously Dad invited Darius along, as Bad News Nan LOVED Darius. Nat didn't quite understand why, but then again she never understood why SHE was Darius's friend either, so eventually she just accepted both facts as STRANGE BUT TRUE.

"Dad, why's Nan actually here?" said Nat, as Dad drove the camp Land Rover into the village. "Don't tell me SHE'S volunteered to help out at the stupid camp too?"

BNN liked volunteering, although her jobs never lasted long.

When she was a hospital visitor, the patients

177

raised money to send her on a cruise. They said they didn't mind where, as long as it was a long one, with chances of icebergs and/or whirlpools/tidal waves/Nan-eating krakens along the way.

When she helped out at a food bank, BNN was banned after making more withdrawals than deposits.

When she volunteered to read newspapers for the blind, she only read the bits she liked – the really gruesome and tragic bits – and then added a lot of gossip she'd heard down at the hairdresser's. Sometimes she mixed them up so everyone thought the prime minister was having an affair with Elsie Gusset from the wet-fish counter at ASDA.

"Nan's here cos there's a funeral," said Dad.

"Makes sense," said Nat. BNN loved funerals. "Is it someone she actually knew or has she just heard they're doing nice cakes afterwards?"

"I think she actually knew the person in this one," said Dad. "She said something about crossing another one out of her address book."

Nat shuddered. BNN's big black address book was more commonly known as THE BOOK OF DOOM.

Because sooner or later, everyone in it met with a horrible fate.

"Promise me you'll never let Nan put me in that address book," said Nat.

Dad chuckled. "I know what you mean," he said. "People in there have as much chance of survival as hedgehogs playing ping-pong on the M1."

"Hey, she put me in there," said Darius, frowning.

Nat cackled. "Bad luck," she said.

BNN was going to meet them in a café in the centre of the village. Lower Totley was one of those towns that guidebooks like to write about. The ones that only really old people like. Because they're ever so quiet.

The place was just a few higgledy-piggledy streets huddled around a large, covered market square. The square had held animal markets every week for hundreds of years and all Nat could think about was how much poop there must still be under it.

As far as Nat could tell, every other shop was either a Ye Olde Tea Shoppe, or a shop selling tea towels. Which had pictures of tea shops on.

There was a large, red-brick library, which had a big sign on it:

CLOSED. SITE OF NEW SUPERSTORE COMING SOON!

Walking to the tea shop, Nat saw a sign which had been crossed out:

PUBLIC BATHS

The only thing that looked like it might be fun was a large boating lake, but it was sad and disused. A bit of pond scum clung to the dirty grey edges.

Chained up at the side of the lake were half-a-dozen fibreglass boats shaped like swans. They must have been pretty and white once, but now they were dirty and unloved. They hung their heads as if to say, *Yeah, don't look. I know we're a bit rubbish these days.*

"They're closed – don't bother queuing," said a wrinkly old lady in a pretty floral headscarf, jabbing Nat with a bony finger. "Something to do with being untidy I should imagine. Huh, you young people. *We* had a war, you know, and we won. We didn't win by being tidy, did we, eh?"

"Erm…" said Nat, who suddenly found herself at the other end of this conversation.

The old lady fixed her with a steely glare. She had surprisingly bright blue eyes. She was wearing a big woolly coat even though it was a hot day.

"Happiest years of my life, the war – apart from the bombs and the disease and the rats and the rationing," said the old lady cheerfully. "And the horrible music. Ooh, I was glad when they invented that hip-hop."

"Right," said Nat, thinking, *Funny, I think everyone in MY town is bonkers, but there's fruit cakes everywhere.*

"What do kids do for fun round here?" Nat asked.

"Leave," said the old lady.

She pointed to a shiny plaque on the wall of a large brick building, formerly the children's library.

It read:

NICE 'N' NEAT COUNTRYSIDE ALLIANCE –
HEAD OFFICES

Nat recognised the name with a shudder. This was where they were going to be horribly shown up on Saturday.

Next to it were five green plaques. Each one said:

WINNER – NICEST 'N' NEATEST TOWN IN THE UK

"Oh, we're tidy all right," said the old lady. "These days they make sure we don't have anything round here that'll make a mess. Including having a good time!"

She wandered off, singing a hip-hop song that was eye-wateringly rude.

"Relative of yours?" Nat asked Darius.

"You do know that was Black Meg, the Lower Snotley Zombie Witch?" said Darius. "They say one drop of her tears cures you of warts."

"You could be a great writer one day," said Dad with a smile, "unless you're locked up for destroying mankind first. It's fifty-fifty with you."

"Take your silly hat off," said Nat, snatching the embarrassing thing from Dad's head. "People are staring."

"What people?" said Dad.

He was right. Lower Totley was almost completely deserted.

"Told you, it's a zombie town," said Darius. "Don't eat any meat pies in this place, that's all I'm saying – they're made of people. THE TASTY BITS."

Bad News Nan was already in the café, EATING A MEAT PIE.

She was on top Bad News Nan form. That is to

say, she hugged Nat, squeezed Darius into her ample bosom until his eyes bulged, wiped his face with a spitty hanky, force-fed him fruit cake and told them all Incredibly Bad News Stories.

Mrs Password from the allotments had rotten ganglions.

Deirdre Instagram's dog had found a shell in the back garden. It was an explosive shell from the war and it blew all her windows out. Worse, she'd just had double glazing put in. At least they got the dog's collar back – it was found three streets away and it still had the name tag on. Deidre was now looking for a new dog with the same name. Lucky.

Mr Toggle at Number 6 had given his life savings to a man on the Internet who said he knew how to make millions of pounds in a day. After Mr Toggle sent the money he'd got an email saying:

JUST TELL IDIOTS ONLINE TO SEND YOU ALL THEIR SAVINGS. HA HA HA.

And Tracey Dangle had won a trip to Disney World.

"Oh. That doesn't actually sound like bad news," said Dad, "so that's nice."

"It wasn't nice for her one bit," said BNN through another mouthful of fruit cake. "She's terrified of mice. She's got a three-month jail sentence for bashing up Mickey with a broom."

Bad News Nan droned to a halt and looked at the counter.

"All the cake's gone," said the café owner with a thin smile. "You've eaten it."

"Lovely funeral this morning," said Bad News Nan, popping her false teeth back in from where she'd put them – in the sugar bowl.

Nat wished she hadn't put sugar in her tea.

"It was my old school friend Judy McSpreader," said BNN. "Funny, hadn't heard from her for years then she found me on the interweb net and got back in touch. Ooh, sad really, I'd only just put her name in my address book."

She took out the leather book of doom from her massive handbag, spilling used tissues on the floor.

"I just need to cross her out," said BNN, with what Nat thought was relish. "Anyone got a black pen?"

BNN spent the next ten minutes telling them what a tragic life her old friend had had, right up until last week when one day she woke up stone dead.

"Probably a relief to her," said BNN. "She was ever so miserable; do you know she only ever saw the gloomy side of things? Death was a relief, I shouldn't wonder."

"You should meet Nat's geography teacher," said Dad. "He'd love you."

"Judy's youngest great-niece is a geography teacher too," said BNN. "I was going to tell you if you'd let me get a word in sideways."

"Sorry, Mum," said Dad with a sigh.

Nat giggled. BNN always made her laugh.

"Yes, she's been away, travelling and teaching

geography abroad. Came back for the funeral. I said to her that I don't know why foreigners need to be taught about foreign countries – they're already there."

Dad looked confused, but Nat just chuckled; she thought Nan's head must be a really interesting place to live in.

"Anyways," continued BNN, "I told her all about you lot. Specially you, Darius."

"Mumph," said Darius, who had been forgotten about.

He was still stuck mid-bosom and had gone a violent shade of purple.

BNN plopped him out and he gasped for air.

"I told her all about your clever little essay. Ooh, she was impressed."

Darius grinned.

Nat frowned.

"She's called Sky. Ooh, she's done ever such a lot," BNN gushed. "Actually, I don't know how she's survived everything. One toe dropped off with frostbite; another one got bitten off by a shark." BNN paused. "Although it might have been a leg. And it might have been a shark, or it might have been a tiger… Anyways, she's very interesting, whatever it is she's done. I missed some of what she was saying – they'd just come out with the ham sandwiches."

Dad sat up. "I could invite her to the camp," he said. "She could give a talk and I could show Mr Dewdrop I've got interesting friends."

"She's not your friend," said Nat.

"Only cos she hasn't met me yet," said Dad confidently. "I'm good at friends."

Nat sighed. It was true – Dad had LOADS of friends. She had no idea why. He was an idiot.

"You didn't get a phone number off her, did you, Mum?" asked Dad.

"Yes, it's somewhere here… Oh, where is it?"

She flicked through the terrible black address book.

Dad, Nat and Darius looked at each other in alarm.

Finally, Nan pulled out a tissue from her sleeve. "Silly me, I wrote her number on a tissue," she said. "Here it is. I'll just add it to my book."

Dad grabbed the number. "No need to put the poor woman in there," he said. "She's suffered enough, what with the frost and the toe-chomping. I'll call her."

But there was no mobile-phone signal in the café so Dad wandered off outside to call her.

Nan watched him, trying to find a signal, through the window. He eventually seemed to find one standing on a park bench in the middle of the town square, holding his phone high above his head.

"What's your father doing now?" said Bad News Nan. "Do you know, Nathalia, my son has spent the last forty years trying to embarrass me? I think it might be because I dropped him on his head as a child."

"It's the phone company he's with," said Nat, as passers-by stood to gawp at Dad. "They're really rubbish but Dad says they're the cheapest."

"There's a reason they're cheap," said Darius, watching Dad's antics.

"Oh, look what's happening now," said Nat. "Some people are throwing change at him – they think he's a street performer."

"Is that why that shopkeeper is trying to move him away with a broom?" said Darius.

"Yeah," said Nat. "The police will probably turn up in a minute, knowing my luck."

Eventually Dad came back to the café, rubbing his tummy.

"Sky sounds nice," he said. "She'll come over and meet us here. Ouch, I'm getting a bruise – that shopkeeper was mean. She said I was a busker and not from round here, and I was making the town untidy."

"You do show me up," said Bad News Nan. She grabbed the waitress's arm. "Have you got kids?" she asked.

"Of course not," said the waitress, "I'm sixteen. Please let go of me."

"Don't have 'em," warned Bad News Nan. "They're just a trial and misery to you, let me tell you."

Dad looked uncomfortable.

Nat giggled. Finally it was Dad's turn to be embarrassed.

"Have I told you about the time he wet the bed when we had that caravan holiday in Wales?" said BNN.

"No, because I've never met you before," said the young waitress, alarmed.

"Mum…" said Dad, "stoppit."

"He was on the top bunk too," said BNN. "I was underneath. Well, I don't need to tell you what *that* was like."

Nat, Darius, and EVERYONE IN THE CAFÉ burst out laughing.

Everyone… except Dad.

"I don't wet the bed any more," said Dad loudly, "just to set the record straight on that one."

"He's such a worry to me," said BNN. "I keep thinking that one day he'll do something useful with his life, but he never does."

"Mum, I'm doing really well," said Dad. "I've won a writing prize, you know."

Nat knew. The Stinker.

"And, er…" said Dad, trying to think of something else useful he'd done. "Oh yes, I've only been at this camp a few days and I'm practically in charge of it now."

"Really?" sniffed BNN.

"Yeah," said Dad. "They love my ideas. They do anything I tell them, really. I basically run it all."

"OOH, aren't you clever? I always knew you'd do well, eventually." She put her arms round him and gave him a big, slobbery, mummy kiss.

Dad went pale.

"He's a good boy really," said BNN, as Dad cringed and Nat guffawed.

And everyone in the café went:

"Aaaah."

Tee-hee, thought Nat. Revenge at last.

CHAPTER SIXTEEN

• • • •

THEY'D JUST FINISHED LUNCH AND DARIUS WAS noisily shovelling his second chocolate pudding down his gullet when Nan's new friend Sky arrived, greeting the waitress and several customers like old friends.

She was a pretty young woman, slender and not very tall, who walked with the kind of grace that suggested hidden strength, like a dancer. She had long brown hair tied in a long ponytail, and the brightest blue eyes. She wore jeans and a T-shirt whose slogan was:

NANGA PARBAT, Man-eater

"Nice to meet you, Miss Parbat," said Dad.

Sky laughed a high, sweet laugh, "Nanga Parbat's the name of the mountain, silly," she giggled. "The *mountain's* the man-eater, not me," she explained.

"Oops," said Dad.

Nat winced.

Sky had an ENORMOUS scar all down her left arm. It was all jagged and looked like…

"Shark," said Sky. "Ex-shark, as it happens." She flashed a set of perfect white teeth.

Nat almost felt sorry for the shark. She reckoned it had never stood a chance. High on Sky's other arm was a delicate tattoo. It was a heart with *DADDY* on.

Sky sat down at the table and took a big swig from a silver hip flask. She wiped her mouth with the back of her hand and belched louder than Darius. Then she giggled unexpectedly.

"Pardon me, terrible habit – from hanging out with the Bedouin in the Sahara too long." She had another swig then put it away.

"God, I hate funerals, don't you?" she said. "In Tibet they just chop you up and leave you to the birds. Don't think we'll get *that* past the Lower Totley Parish Council though."

Nat decided there and then that this was the most AWESOME woman she'd ever met.

They introduced themselves.

Darius must like her, thought Nat – he wiped his hand before shaking hers.

"Sky. What a lovely name," said Dad.

"Mum called me Sky because it was the first thing she saw after I was born. It's a good luck thing for many tribespeople. I mean, she was from Lower Totley, but still, she'd seen a documentary or something and thought it was cool."

They all laughed.

"Dad had taken her to an open-air pop festival when she was nearly nine months pregnant, the idiot. Said it would be good for me to hear music in the womb."

"Sounds like the sort of daft thing my dad would do," said Nat.

"Anyway, halfway through a particularly vigorous drum solo, I just sort of arrived." Sky smiled. "Mum woke up flat on her back, staring at the sky. That's how I got my name."

"That's brilliant," said Nat.

"It was fortunate too, because the very *next* thing

Mum saw was the lead singer of the Electric Prunes and he was called Bogshed."

Nan announced she had to get back to her B&B for a lie-down because all the cake had given her wind.

Everyone who knew Nan dived for the exit.

They had a little time before heading back to the camp and Sky offered to take them on a guided tour of the town.

"It won't take long," she said. "There's not much left."

Nat detected a note of sadness in her voice.

"Zombies?" said Darius.

Sky laughed. "Yeah, you could say that," she joked, "but not in the way you mean."

She pointed to the building that was now the head office of the Nice 'N' Neat Countryside Alliance.

"This town used to be great fun," she said. "When I was growing up, there were fairs and carnivals and parades. There were fireworks and street parties and even a festival of rotten fruit-throwing."

"Rotten fruit-throwing?" said Nat. "That sounds like what happens when my dad plays the ukulele."

Dad laughed. "She's right," he admitted.

"My dad used to organise everything," Sky continued. "He was one of those dads."

"Ooh, I know what you mean," said Nat, looking at her dad.

"Did you have the Green Bogey Festival?" said Dad. "I bet you did. I've been told he's very important round here."

"I've never heard of the Green Bogey," said Sky.

"Told you so, Dad, you spanner," said Nat. "Carry on, Sky."

"But then my dad died, and not long after that the tidy people turned up and everything that caused a mess was closed down. Now the town just wins the tidiest town award every year, but it could also win the most boring."

"Is that why you went travelling?" asked Nat.

"Maybe." Sky shrugged. "You know, this coming Saturday is the day we used to have the carnival, but all that happens now is that everyone goes to the town hall and watches videos of previous carnivals and then they get a talk on how messy it was."

"Not much of a carnival," said Darius, who liked mess.

Sky shook her head. "It's super rubbish. They're

saying the high point of Saturday's carnival will be looking at a couple of geography projects done by stupid kids. Can you imagine?"

"Yes," said Nat, "I can imagine. I can imagine it'll be even more rubbish for the stupid kids."

Sky slapped her forehead. "Oh, I get it, YOU'RE the stupid – I mean, you're the kids! Sorry, I'm sure you won't be rubbish."

"No, I will be," said Nat glumly.

"Listen," said Dad. "Never mind THEM being rubbish – I'm not looking too good at the moment. Sky, I need your help. Will you come and talk to the kids at our camp please? Only, I'm trying to make a good impression on one of the Nice 'N' Neat Countryside people, so if you do come, please don't say anything horrible about them, even if they are horrible. It could be dead embarrassing. Not for me, but for Nathalia," he added hastily. "She's oversensitive about getting embarrassed. Probably her hormones. She's quite a little girl for her age really, aren't you, love?"

He gave Nat a big dad squeeze.

"Gerroff, not in public," said Nat.

"Oh yes, you won that competition, didn't you?"

said Sky, looking at Darius. "I recognise your photo from the newspaper now. You're the clever essay writer."

"It's a gift," said Darius.

"Yes, MY gift, you cheaty chimp," snapped Nat.

"You did it TOGETHER? How adorable," said Sky.

Nat went red.

Darius put his fingers down his throat and made retching noises.

They had ended up standing next to the closed boating lake. There was a little neat sign that explained it was due to be concreted over and turned into an ornamental fountain. It also said:

NO SPLASHING ALLOWED

"I miss having a special friend," said Sky.

With horror, Nat realised she was talking about HER AND DARIUS BAGLEY.

"The thing about travelling is, you meet hundreds of people but you can feel ever so alone," Sky said.

"Tell me about it," said a sad voice Nat recognised.

Mr Keane was sitting in one of the fibreglass swan boats, reading a book.

No one had noticed him because he was one of

those people no one notices.

"Hello," he said. "I had to get away from camp for a bit. Don't tell anyone. I just said all that healthy eating had given me the runs. It's not much of a fib."

Mr Keane sighed and chucked his book in the lake. As it sank, Nat read the title: *How to Be Happy*.

That's going well then, she thought.

"Who am I kidding?" he said. "It's a big fat lie. I never get the galloping trots. I once ate a whole camel's head with no ill effects."

"When did you eat a whole camel's head?" said Sky, who sounded like she didn't believe him.

"When I was the guest at a wedding feast in the High Atlas mountains," said Mr Keane, noticing Sky for the first time and going the sort of red that Nat usually went.

"If you say so," said Sky.

Something about her tone of voice made Mr Keane hop out of the boat. He looked cross.

"Look here," he said, "just because all my pupils think I'm rubbish—"

"We don't," said Nat.

"We do," said Darius.

"…and all the teachers think I'm rubbish—"

"They don't," said Nat.

"They do," said Dad, feeling a bit left out.

"…it doesn't mean EVERYONE can think I'm rubbish, even women…" he paused for a second, "…even women as beautiful as you."

Sky took a step back in surprise.

"I had dreams once," said Mr Keane. "When I couldn't get into vet school, I decided to write. I was going to write a novel about a man who wanted to write a novel, so I went to live with the Berber people in the mountains in Morocco."

"Why?" asked Dad.

"Because that's what the man in my novel did," said Mr Keane.

"Was your novel any good?" said Nat.

"I never finished it," said Mr Keane. "I just wrote a diary of my adventures. I published it myself and I think I sold two copies. One was to my mum."

"And the other one was to me!" said Sky, eyes widening.

She rummaged around in her backpack and pulled out a tatty, well-thumbed copy of:

My Life Trying to Write a Novel in the Atlas Mountains with the Berber by IAN MICHAELMAS KEANE.

"This book literally saved my life," she said in amazement. "I picked it up for five pence at a car boot sale. It's so hilariously funny, it kept me going when I was at my most miserable."

"It's not supposed to be funny," muttered Mr Keane, but Sky didn't hear.

"Oh, remember the time when you rescued that dog but it turned out to be a giant rat?"

"Not funny. It almost had my finger off."

"Or the time you forgot that a Bedouin prince has to give you anything you say you like, and you told him how much you liked his wife?"

"Extremely embarrassing."

"And you must tell everyone about the sandstorm, the camel, and the inflatable penguin."

"No I must not!" said Mr Keane. He got so agitated he lost his footing and fell backwards…

… straight into the boating lake.

"You're still funny!" shouted Sky, grabbing him and easily dragging him out.

"No one's ever said that before," said Mr Keane, spitting out a water beetle.

"No one tells you," said Dad. "No one recognises comic genius until you're old and not funny any more. That's how it happens. Look at me – no one thinks I'm funny."

"Wrong, Dad," said Nat. "EVERYONE thinks you're funny."

"That's so sweet," said Sky, but winking at Nat to show she knew EXACTLY what Nat meant.

"Oh heck, look at the time," said Dad. "We're running late and I can't get another black mark."

"I can't go back like this," said the sopping Mr Keane.

"You can clean up at my flat," said Sky, "and borrow some clean clothes."

"Nothing's a problem for you, is it?" said Mr Keane.

"Never met one yet that can't be beat!" Sky laughed.

Mr Keane suddenly straightened up. He turned to Dad and said, "Tell them at the camp that I'm worse, and I've gone into town to buy some stomach medicine and a cork. I may be gone some time."

"I see you're a rebel," said Sky, impressed.

"I am," said Mr Keane, puffing himself up, "although I have to be back at camp tonight as it's my turn to help with the washing-up."

"I'll get him back in time," laughed Sky, turning to Dad. "Now, what fun have you got lined up this afternoon?"

"Eeek, we're late for it," said Dad, dragging the kids back to the car.

"Where ARE we off to now, Dad?" said Nat, as Dad whizzed her and Darius along winding country roads in the Land Rover.

"I'm trying to concentrate," said Dad. "I'm looking for a riding school. It's the next camp activity."

"Like the one we just passed?" said Nat.

Dad slammed on the brakes. "You might have said," he complained, crunching gears and turning round.

He found the entrance, revved up the earth drive and skidded to a halt by a large iron barn.

The other children were already there, all kitted out in riding gear. One group of riders, led by Mr Bungee and, next to him, little suck-up Plum, were already trotting off into the woods.

"We so love pony-trekking," said Plum excitedly, clip-clopping past Nat and Penny on a sleek white pony. "Our school has its own ponies, you know."

"Course you do," said Nat pleasantly, "but that's only because your unicorns flew away."

"Unicorns can't fly, silly," said Penny. "That's just a myth."

Mr B laughed sarcastically.

Plum rode past, giggling. "You girls are SO adorable," she said.

"Yeah, aren't we just," said Nat through gritted teeth. She elbowed Penny sharply in the ribs.

But Nat couldn't stay annoyed for very long. She had just got a waft of that lovely smell of hay and warm horse.

"Stop being grumpy with me. You told me you like ponies," said Penny.

Nat just grunted. She DID like ponies, but she didn't want to admit it in front of THAT school.

"You're late. You got a horse yet?" said Darius, in a riding hat a size too big for him.

"Not yet," said Nat, jogging to the tack room to get riding gear on.

She ran past Dad, who was being given a stern talking-to by Mr Dewdrop for driving into the yard so fast.

"Won't be long," said Dad. "Only, I've got to drive the Land Rover again and prove to Mr Dewdrop that I don't always drive like a... What was it you said?"

Mr Dewdrop said something.

"Well, never mind what he said. Back soon. Have fun riding."

Dad drove off VERY CAREFULLY with Mr Dewdrop in the car, taking notes.

Darius shouted something to Nat, but – in her haste and what with Dad's telling-off – she missed it. She thought she heard "evil" and "plan", but most things Darius said involved those words, so she wasn't too bothered.

She should have been bothered.

CHAPTER SEVENTEEN

• • • •

NAT STARTED TO GET BOTHERED WHEN SHE SAW Darius deep in an argument with Mr Rainbow, who was taking the riding session. Nat couldn't quite hear what was going on because Miss Slippy was putting her riding hat on and Nat was wriggling like an eel.

"Oh, ow, that's my hair!" said Nat.

"Oh, do keep still," snapped Miss Slippy, "we haven't got all day. I knew you were a problem child – I can tell by looking at your father."

Thanks again, Dad, thought Nat, keeping a bit more still but with an ear strained for Darius.

"All these ponies are for babies," said Darius.

"We need something bigger and better for Buttface."

"Who?" said Mr Rainbow.

"What's he saying?" said Nat, who'd heard her horrible nickname.

"Keep still while I put your hat on straight," tutted Miss Slippy, fussing with her strap.

"Ow, that's my hair caught in the strap AGAIN," complained Nat. "Lemme go, I need to hear this."

But Miss Slippy wouldn't let her go so she only half-heard the conversation taking place about her.

"The only big pony here is Satan," said a stable girl, coming over to help Mr Rainbow. "I mean, actually he's called Stan. Satan's just a silly nickname."

From inside the stalls came a deep whinny, and the sound of crashing hoofs.

Another stable girl came flying out of the door.

"That's it," shouted the stable girl, throwing down a brush, dusting herself off and stomping away. "I don't care what you do with that flipping monster horse. Put him in a tin of cat food for all I care! I'm not brushing him any more – he's a menace."

"He sounds perfect," said Darius, eyes gleaming. "She likes a challenge."

"Who?" said Mr Rainbow.

"He means Nathalia," said Miss Hunny doubtfully.

Darius stuck his head around the stable door.

A whinny shook the air.

"Oh yeah, he's perfect," said Darius, pulling his head back.

"What's going on?" said Nat, finally scuttling over, still adjusting her hat. "I heard my name. What are you up to?"

Darius whispered, "It's the evil plan. It's going brilliantly. Don't spoil it."

"Oh, OK," said Nat, "if you're sure." SHE wasn't even sure, but she knew her future school life was hanging in the balance…

"Nathalia, come back. Your hat still isn't on properly," Miss Slippy called from the stable. "If you fall on your head you'll lose what little brain you have."

Nat looked at Darius then ran back to the tack room.

"Nat should get that pony," said Darius firmly. "She's really good at riding. Oh come on, trust me – I'm leader and everything."

Mr Rainbow sniggered. "I'm not sure you can trust a boy like him," he said.

"There's nothing wrong with our little Darius Bagley," said Miss Hunny defensively.

She grabbed him and started to give him a hug. Then she stopped.

"Heavens, you're sticky," she said, quickly letting him go.

"Besides, Nathalia is Darius's very best friend," Miss H added, wiping her hands down her jeans.

"If you say so," said Mr Rainbow.

"Yes, I do say so," said Miss H, "so there."

She turned to Darius and looked him in the eye. This was rare: most people thought looking him in the eye was bad luck. Some people even claimed he could suck out their souls through his eyeballs, but Miss Hunny didn't QUITE believe that.

"Are you absolutely sure Nathalia can handle this horrible horse?" she said.

"Course," said Darius innocently, "she's got ribbons and medals and everything. I thought everybody knew."

"Oh my. It seems you don't know the children in your own class," said Mr Rainbow. "That's not very good teaching, is it?"

"That's ridiculous," said Miss Hunny, stung.

"Now, come to mention it, I think I've seen Nathalia's riding ribbons. In her own house. That's right: I'm not just a teacher, I'm a friend. That's what our school is like."

"What is that dreadful woman talking about?" said Miss Eyre. "The children are *our friends*?"

"I don't like the teachers, never mind the children," said Miss Austen.

"I wouldn't have thought anyone from your school could manage a horse like this," said Mr Rainbow, just as Nat came back.

"Oh yeah? Just watch her," said Miss Hunny, who was fed up with the snooty teachers. "Nathalia, show them what you can do."

By now all the children had gathered round to watch. A braver stable girl went into the stalls and led the fierce pony out.

The children went:

"OOH."

Nathalia gulped. It was MASSIVE.

Stan was less like a pony, more like a warhorse. And not a nice warhorse who would actually rather be munching daisies in a quiet field and trotting tamely with schoolkids. Oh no. One of those bonkers and really grumpy warhorses who wanted to be headbutting tanks and dodging bullets and trampling enemy soldiers.

"Satan, Satan," came the cry from the kids.

"You're not helping," muttered Nat.

She looked at Darius. "What have you done?" she said.

"Shush," said Darius, "this is part of my evil plan. Soon, everyone will think you totally hate me."

"Why?" asked Nat.

"Because you're about to have a terrible time, thanks to me." Darius grinned.

Before Nat could say anything, Miss Hunny grabbed her and started pushing her on to the big horse.

"Ow, Miss," complained Nat, clambering on.

"Show them what you can do," Miss Hunny whispered, still pushing her. "Don't let me down now."

"I can't do anything," said Nat, getting her feet caught on the stirrups. She wriggled about, still trying to get on the saddle.

"Nonsense," said Miss Hunny, pushing hard, "Darius says you've got ribbons and rosettes."

"I won a donkey race when I was eight," said Nat. "Does that count?"

"Oh," said Miss Hunny, "maybe not. I think Darius might have been naughty. I suppose you should come down."

But it was too late. With all the pushing, Nat was now on the horse.

But she was FACING BACKWARDS.

"There's something wrong," said Miss Hunny.

"Get me down! I'm high up and it's scary," shouted Nat.

Stan the horse bucked.

"Stoppit, bad horsey," said Nat, automatically slapping its rear end.

Which was the worst thing to do.

With a huge whinny, the big grumpy horse took off with Nat facing the wrong way, bouncing like a sack of bouncy potatoes on a bouncy castle. Only less elegantly.

"Is she all right?" said Mr Rainbow, alarmed, as Stan raced off into a field.

"She likes doing tricks," said Miss Hunny. "*You* might say it's showing off, but our school supports its—"

"HEEELLLLLPPPPPP!" shouted Nat.

"She just loves getting attention," said Miss Hunny, advancing towards Darius, who took off like a rocket.

Meanwhile, Nat was clinging on for dear life as Stan, loving the freedom, raced through the fields, overtaking the line of ponies that had set out first.

The children riding cheered as Nat shot past.

Nat was clinging on to Stan's tail. Her head was bouncing in and out of the black bushy thing. The horse reached a fence, turned back and headed for the yard.

"It smells like horse bum," yelled Nat.

"Keep your mouth closed," yelled Darius, as she flew past.

"Yuk!" yelled Nat. "I hate you, Bagley. I really do."

"And I should bop you on the nose," said Rufus, dodging out of the way of the wild horse.

"Bop off," said Darius.

"Maybe later," said Rufus. "Consider yourself warned."

Darius ignored him.

"Hold tight," shouted Mr Bungee, riding his horse to the rescue like a cowboy.

He caught up with Stan, grabbed the reins and brought him under control within seconds.

Gratefully, Nat slid off, legs trembling.

"If it was up to me," shouted Mr Bungee, "I'd send you home right now. You could have got yourself hurt, messing about like that. You're an embarrassment to your whole school."

Shamefully, she trudged into the tack room to

take off her riding kit.

A few seconds later, Darius popped his head around the door.

"Perfect," he said.

Nat threw her hat at him.

Nat ignored Darius for the rest of the day.

At dinner she glared daggers at him. As he went past her in the dining hall, she casually stuck out her foot and sent him flying across the floor.

"You have to admit," said Penny, over the sound of Darius clattering to a halt, "that you're acting like you hate Darius ever so well. You could be in the next school play. I totally believe it."

"Hmmm," said Nat. "Thing is, I'm not just acting. Anyway, I dunno if he's been doing this as part of his evil scheme or if he's ACTUALLY getting me back for all the times I've, er—"

"Pinched him, punched him, made him eat grass, locked him in the loo, hidden his trunks at the swimming gala, called him chimpy, and set fire to his tie in chemistry? Just for a few examples?" said Penny.

"You're getting on my nerves too," snapped Nat,

and stomped outside to have a think.

She sat on a log by herself, listening to the birds saying goodnight to each other and wishing she had a bird scarer because they were SO FLIPPING LOUD.

She began to wonder if she was QUITE such a good friend as she would have liked to be. She was a kind-hearted soul deep down.

I spend a lot of time thinking about making new friends, she thought, *but I wonder if I should take a tiny bit more care of my old ones?*

Then she felt a bit sick because she hadn't got much of a project to show on Saturday because all her time had been taken up with *schemes*.

She was about to decide to be a better friend AND to work harder, but she forgot all about that because she saw a little car with a flower on the side pull up.

Inside it were MR KEANE AND SKY.

AND MR KEANE WAS LAUGHING!

Nat dodged behind the log, out of sight. She watched as they sat talking *for ages*. They were still there as the light faded and Nat reluctantly headed back to her yurt and sleeping bag.

CHAPTER EIGHTEEN

....

"REMEMBER OUR PLAN," WHISPERED DARIUS, AS they walked into the classroom the next morning.

"To act like I hate you. How can I forget? I'm totally on my guard against you," said Nat, just as Darius tripped her up.

"WAAH!" shouted Nat, as she careered into a big spinning globe.

"EEEK!" she yelled, as she was whizzed around it twice, picking up speed.

"NOOO!" she squeaked, as she was flung straight into the arms...

... of Rufus.

Who caught her easily. All the children cheered and some made slurpy, kissy-kissy noises.

Nat went a deeper shade of red than she had ever deep-redded before.

Which was a pretty deep red.

"You really are a rotter, Bagley," said Rufus, releasing Nat.

Darius just shrugged and went into a cupboard.

"What IS he doing in there?" said the St Scrofula's boy.

Nat shrugged. "No one likes to ask."

It was Mr Keane's turn again to present a lesson. Was it Nat's imagination, or was he looking a bit less like a wretched hobo and more like a proper teacher?

"Has he had a shave?" she asked Penny.

"Dunno," said Penny, "I'm still looking at his shirt. There's no bean stains down it."

"Good morning, young geographers," said Mr Keane. "AND WHAT A GREAT MORNING IT IS."

"Has he been drinking?" whispered Miss A to Miss E. "There's something different about him."

"I think he's smiling," said Miss Eyre. "That's odd."

"There's a ridge of high pressure moving in overhead, which means warm sunny weather – that's geography – and today we'll be taking the B234 road going north-east – that's more geography – to see the FUTURE OF THIS PLANET – and that's MORE GEOGRAPHY THAN YOU CAN HANDLE!"

Mr Keane did a happy little dance and pressed a button on his phone. Princess Boo blared out. It was her classic hit:

"*I'm so happy because I'm so happy. Get so happy too.*"

"Take the morning off, gang," said Mr Keane. "Meet me after lunch. Cancel your afternoon appointments, clear your schedules, we're going TO THE MOON!"

Dr Nobel strode up to him and turned off the music. "I'm making a citizen's arrest. Your teacher has gone mad. Call for the nurse."

"Chill, Daddy-o," said Mr Keane. "All I mean is, I've got us all an invite to THE MOON HOUSE."

"What?" said Nat.

Penny shrugged.

Dr Nobel laughed. "Now I know you've flipped

your lid!" he said. "No one can see the Moon House. It's geography's holy grail, a quest that's impossible."

"Wrong cue, ball head," said Mr Keane, "and I'll prove it to you. Everyone, meet me at the minibuses after lunch." And he skipped out of the room.

There was a stunned silence.

Dad looked at Nat and made a twirly motion with his fingers next to his head.

As they trooped out, Nat found herself talking to Rufus.

"What's happened to your teacher?" he said.

"I have a horrible feeling it's cos he has to teach us," said Nat, "and we've sent him round the bend. It's like those soldiers we read about that spend too long in a trench. One day, they're fighting like normal; the next, they put their underpants on their head and say they're the fairy from the top of the Christmas tree."

"You're really funny," said Rufus. "Has anyone ever told you?"

"All the time," said Dad, butting in. "Of course, she gets it from me. Rufus, I hope you'll be taking one of my comedy-writing classes one day." He paused. "Oh, actually, I'm only going to be running those for young offenders. Still, if you commit a terrible crime you can come for free."

Nat fled from Dad's burbling into the open air, dragging Penny with her.

"So, you and posho Rufus... What's going on, girlfriend?" said Penny, in the way that Princess Boo spoke in every episode of her reality show, *The Princess Boo Diaries*.

"Nothing's going on, and stop talking like that," said Nat crossly.

"Don't you mean, talk to the hand, the face isn't listening?" said Penny.

"No, I mean, shuddup or I'll force-feed you a cowpat," said Nat. "Nothing is going on except for Darius's evil plan. He has to pretend to be horrible and I have to pretend to like Rufus. Remember?"

Penny grinned. "That's not an evil plan," she teased. "Darius IS horrible, and you DO like Rufus."

"If you insist on being ridiculous, I'm not conversing with you," said Nat, walking away, nose in the air.

"You even sound like Rufus now," said Penny.

Nat ran at her, ready for throttling.

"EEEK!" squealed Penny, taking flight.

Class 8H now had "project study time".

Nat was aware that the kids from the rival school were huddled in a hot classroom, working hard on their project. She was happy enough that Darius would spoil it, so she reckoned she didn't have to stress too much about what they were going to do as their project just yet.

Besides, it was a lovely day, and she was quite keen to join in a conversation that Julia Pryde, Peaches Bleary and Sally Bung were having about eyebrows.

Out of the corner of her eye, she saw a large white van arrive, and the St Scrofula's teachers helped Mr Bungee take delivery of something in a huge wooden crate. But she soon forgot all about it because Peaches Bleary was asking their opinion on whether she should get her eyebrows waxed or threaded.

Nat saw Penny sketching something in her pad, off by herself. She wanted to invite her to join them but knew Penny wasn't very good at girly talk, so left her alone. *It's kinder that way*, thought Nat.

Everyone was buzzing at lunch.

One of two things was about to happen.

The children had found out what the Moon House was: the country's only HOUSE IN AN ECO DOME. It had been built by a reclusive dot-com billionaire who had got fed up with the rotten world that had given him all those billions. Now he lived in a dome, surrounded by half the world's plants and animal species. Usually he wouldn't let anyone else have a peek, so going there would be AWESOME.

And if they weren't doing that then it meant Mr Keane had finally gone crackers and they were about to see him carted off by the men in white coats. Which was ALSO AWESOME.

Either way, the kids were well happy.

They all assembled in the car park, waiting to see which option it was.

Some of the more evil-minded kids were disappointed when Mr Keane turned up looking cheerful and SANE.

A little car with a flower on the side screeched up. Sky waved from the window and told the driver to follow her.

On the minibus, Mr Keane bagsied a seat next to Nat.

"Hello, project leader," said Mr Keane cheerfully.

Nat felt sick. She hadn't been doing much project-leading – more 'someone else's project-destroying'.

"Today," said Mr Keane, "is the day we're going to come up with an idea for our project. Being at the eco dome should inspire us."

"That's nice," said Nat, "but does it mean we have to do any work?"

"It's not work if it's something you love," said Mr Keane. He grinned a broad smile. "We're the first people to get an invite to Professor Paradise's home, thanks to me and you. That'll look pretty good in our project, right?"

"Am I going to have to, like, write about it?" said Nat.

Mr Keane ignored her. "I must thank your nan for introducing me to Sky. She's totally AMAZING."

Ew, thought Nat.

"Did you know she's Professor Paradise's god-daughter? She's helped him collect some of his weirder specimens. Sky's going to ask him to give us something really rare for our presentation on

Saturday. How cool is that?"

Cool, thought Nat darkly. *But my plan is cooler.*
Mwah-ha-haaa.

CHAPTER NINETEEN

• • • •

NAT HAD TO ADMIT, THE DOME HOME WAS... AMAZING.

It was deep in a hidden, secret valley. It was so well hidden that only the most intrepid people would ever find it. Once the minibuses were parked, Sky led the children down steep stone paths that skirted an ugly quarry before...

There it was.

A great glass dome, surrounded by the most beautiful flowering plants and trees anyone had ever seen.

Everyone gasped, even the stuck-up St Scrofula's teachers.

They entered through a sort of air lock, which opened automatically. Then they were all sprayed with something to kill bugs. Finally, they were allowed into an enormous, magical garden.

"Well done, Mr Bumolé," said Mr Dewdrop to Dad, as they walked through the flowering loveliness. "I can't believe Mr Keane organised this. Tell me, was it you really? Am I right?"

Dad then did that thing that drove Nat nuts: he was LOVELY. It drove her nuts because it made life very confusing – she never knew whether to be cross with him or to hug him.

"Nope," said Dad, looking at the small figure of Mr Keane at the back of the group, "it's genuinely all Mr Keane's doing. He knows some amazing people."

"Well done, Mr Keane," said Flora Marling, which meant everyone else immediately chimed in to praise him. There was even a round of applause.

Mr Keane looked a bit surprised. "Well, I, er," he said.

"Don't be modest," said Dad, "otherwise everyone might think you might be a rubbish geography teacher who hates everything to do with geography, teaching, children – and, indeed, life."

"Well, I do like to inspire my children," Mr Keane said.

Nat noticed Sky brush past him and give his hand a quick squeeze.

Ew, ew, EW, she thought.

She slid over to Dad. "What are you doing?" she said, out of Mr Keane's earshot, "I thought you needed to get back in Mr Dewdrop's good books? That was your chance."

"I can't take the credit for someone else's idea. Besides, I think Mr Keane needs it more than me," said Dad kindly, and Nat felt the familiar rush of warmth for him.

She tried to hold it back because it was usually followed by Dad doing something ESPECIALLY embarrassing, like kissing her in public, aaagh.

"You can almost believe in fairies in a place like this," said Nat, as they walked to the Moon House through paradise.

"ALMOST?" said Penny, shaking her head.

"He's got the smelliest plant in the world in here," said Darius, as they wandered through the bright glade of the enchanted forest, towards the big, gleaming, glass dome. "It's called a corpse flower."

"Trust you to know that," said Nat, who was entranced by the hundreds of tiny glittering insects being chased and eaten by the beautiful, delicate birds. "Oh look, even terrifying kill-or-be-killed nature looks pretty here."

"It's a big orchid that only sprouts once in a hundred years," said Darius. "It kills most people who sniff it stone dead. Those who survive say it smells like rotting zombie fart."

"Stop it with the zombies," snapped Nat. "And try to look intelligent – we're trying to help Mr Keane look a bit less rubbish."

"Thanks," said Mr Keane, who had overheard.

"I didn't know anything about this place," sniffed Dr Nobel to Miss Slippy, as they bustled past, "and I know almost everything about geography."

Nat was pleased to see Mr Bungee didn't look happy either. "Obviously we've got better gardens in New Zealand," he said, "but I have to admit, it's not bad, not bad at all."

"Welcome to the future of our Earth!" boomed a big voice.

Sky gave the man with the big voice a hug.

Professor Paradise was a huge man who resembled a tree, from his big twisty beard right down to his long, root-like, bare, brown toes.

The tree man looked nervously at all his guests, like he wasn't sure what to say next.

"He's not used to people," Sky said.

"That's fine," muttered Miss Eyre. "Most of 8H aren't people."

Miss Austen chuckled.

I hope there's some man-eating plants in here, thought Nat. *I'll feed you to them.*

With some prompting from his god-daughter, Professor Paradise showed the visitors around the main features of his dome. There was water recycling and solar panels, hydroponics and other dull stuff.

"Got any crocodiles?" said Darius.

"They would upset the delicate balance of nature," said the professor.

"If you're worried about that, you shouldn't have let Darius in," joked Nat.

"I do have some interesting animals in here,"

Professor Paradise said, leading them all to a huge wooden building near a lake.

A sign above the door said:

VIVARIUM

"We don't do Latin," sneered Julia Pryde. "Unlike some kids I know."

"And aren't you lucky?" muttered Plum, pushing past.

Well said, thought Nat, surprising herself.

Inside there were hundreds of glass tanks containing thousands of amazing reptiles and amphibians, all living in total luxury with their own favourite plants. The tanks were of all shapes and sizes, and there were countless rows of them, all lit with soft, solar-powered UV lights. The biggest tank even had a towering, full-sized tree in! The huge room was warm, and hummed quietly.

"Don't touch," said the professor. "These are my pride and joy – many collected by Sky here – and they're some of the most endangered species on Earth."

Darius looked bored.

"And some of the most dangerous too," said Sky.

Darius looked interested.

"This one might be my favourite," said the professor, indicating a modestly-sized tank filled with leaves, moss, and a big branch. Two little brightly-coloured frogs were sunning themselves under the lights.

"Peruvian zombie-frogs," he said.

Darius was SO interested.

"For years only a legend. But I proved they were real."

"Well, I led the expedition," said Sky. "They were quite tricky to find, by the way."

"The tribespeople say one drop of the juice from a squeezed frog turns enemies to zombies."

"There was a flipping big swamp I had to get through," continued Sky. "Not to mention a ravine, mud spouts, and that flood."

"I know how you feel," sympathised Nat. "No one listens to us – it's cos we're girls."

"I heard *that*," said Professor Paradise.

Nat and Sky chuckled.

After the tour they were allowed to wander around the garden, as long as they promised not to break anything.

Nat was so mesmerised she failed to notice that

she'd been walking on her own for a while. She heard footsteps behind her.

It was Rufus.

"I got lost," fibbed Rufus.

"Right," said Nat.

They walked for a bit in silence.

"Can I ask you something?" he said eventually. "Why is everyone unfriendly to us? Is it just because of the school we go to?"

"No," fibbed Nat.

"Yes it is. We're used to it. But it's not fair, you know – we never asked to go there. And no one hates you because of YOUR school."

Nat looked at the ground. She was starting to feel a teeny bit bad.

"Have you thought it might not be so nice for *us* having to be so flipping perfect all the time?" Rufus asked.

She hadn't. Not one bit. Nat grunted, wishing he'd shut up. Because she was now starting to feel GUILTY.

"Last year a girl called Emma Nutbush got three Bs in her exams and the teachers wouldn't speak to her for a week. She made the front page of the school newspaper. It said: 'What's the difference between a hive and Emma Nutbush?' And inside it said: 'Hives have fewer bees.'"

Nat giggled. "Oh, that's rotten," she said. "Poor Emma Nutbush."

"Yeah, plus she's called Nutbush," laughed Rufus.

"Could be worse," said Nat. "My name's terrible too."

"Join the club. I'm Rufus Bojangles-Chutney," said Rufus B-C. "I want to play up front for Spurs – can you imagine *that* on the commentary?"

Nat laughed.

"And I had a lucky escape. My dad wanted to call me Gaylord, like my older cousin Gaylord Bojangles-Chutney."

"What does he do?" said Nat, shoulders shaking.

"Doesn't matter what he does, he has a terrible time. He could be the first Gaylord on Mars, but everyone's still gonna be laughing at him."

By now Nat was laughing like a drain.

"Wait there. Back in a tick," said Rufus, dashing off.

She heard a hissing noise coming from behind a nearby apple tree.

It was evil ninja Darius, hiding in the long lush grass, crawling like a snake.

"It's going brilliantly. Now ask him about his secret project. Go on," hissed Darius, "while his defences are down."

"Don't want to. Shuddup," whispered Nat. "I don't think he's completely horrible any more."

"You have to," said Darius. "I heard your dad ask Dr Nobel about admission forms earlier."

EEEK, thought Nat.

Just then Rufus came back and Darius slunk off back into the grass.

Rufus was holding a long stalk with many pink and purple little flowers attached.

"This is called a Stinking Christopher," he said, "but just cos it's got a horrible name doesn't mean it's not… you know… nice."

"It is nice," said Nat.

"You can have it if you want, but it's not like I'm giving it to you or anything," he said, shuffling his feet. "And it's a branch, not flowers, so I'm not giving you flowers, OK?"

Nat took it. "Thanks," she said.

In the grass she heard Darius making quiet kissing noises and decided enough was enough.

"So, our stupid projects for Saturday," she said. "Ours isn't very good. I think we're just gonna draw a map of Lower Snotley or something. It's rubbish but that's cos it's Darius Bagley's idea. He's such an UTTER AND TOTAL CHIMP that it'll be a disaster."

"He is a bit of a chimp, isn't he?" laughed Rufus.

"Oh, a baboon," said Nat. "I think he's even got a purple bottom. It's fat enough to be a baboon's bum."

"It matches his face," said Rufus.

"I think it was trending on Twitter," said Nat really loudly. "Hashtag Darius Bagley has a face like a monkey's rear end. An ugly monkey's rear end too."

"He eats his bogeys," said Rufus.

"He eats other people's bogeys," shouted Nat. "He says they help the worms go down easier."

"Is he actually human?" said Rufus.

"Good question," said Nat, enjoying herself. "Is Darius Bagley human? Some say he's a failed lab experiment, but I think he's a successful lab experiment – in creating the most horrible creature in the world."

"Why do you hang around with him then?"

"I don't, not really. You must have seen us arguing. And look what he did to me at the riding school. He thinks I won't get him back for that but OH YES, I WILL."

"I think you feel sorry for him. Gosh, you are nice."

"I am. I am so nice. Bagley finds it hard to make friends and that really bothers him. All he thinks about is making friends and where he is on the popularity ladder. AND HE'S RIGHT AT THE

BOTTOM OF IT, THE LITTLE STINKER." She paused to catch her breath.

"I almost feel sorry for him," she continued, feeling super-sneaky, "I mean, he thinks he'll be popular if our project beats yours but it won't because it's totally rubbish. It's about longshore drift or sediment – I don't even know. He's basically making a big mud pie. What a loser."

She put her hand over her mouth like she'd said too much.

"Oh no, I shouldn't have told you our project! Oh never mind, I trust you not to say anything."

Rufus looked like he was making a big decision.

Finally, he said, "Our project's flipping awesome, to be honest. You see, Plum's auntie works for the Met Office. You know, the weather office."

Yes, I do actually GO to school, even if it hasn't got its own swimming pool and helipad, thought Nat.

Her face must have given her away because Rufus apologised immediately.

"Sorry, course you know. Anyway, she's lent us a weather balloon so we can track changes in the jet stream. We've hidden it in Dr Nobel's yurt. We'll have a live video feed down to the town hall on Saturday. With a bit of luck we can link up with the International Space Station too."

Nat looked a bit sick.

"But I'm sure your map will be just as good as our awesome project," he said hastily. "I won't tell anyone about your map. I can keep a secret. Especially," he added, running off, "if it's *your* secret."

Nat felt terrible, then an apple clonked her on the back of the head.

"Baboon's bum?" said Darius, standing up. "Hashtag monkey's purple bum? He wants to make friends? He eats other people's bogeys?"

"I was just carrying out your evil plan," she said lightly, munching on the apple. "He has to believe we've fallen out."

"You were pretty convincing," said Darius.

"Yeah, wasn't I?" said Nat. "Mmm, this apple is delicious."

It tasted of… victory.

Disaster struck five seconds later. "One of my frogs is missing!" yelled a furious Professor Paradise, thrashing through the undergrowth. "Some fool has opened the tank and let it out."

"Which one?" said Sky, looking worried.

Everyone began to run towards the mad professor. Actually, the HOPPING mad professor.

"One of the zombie-frogs," he said. "It'll take me ages to find it again."

"Again?" muttered Sky. "You didn't find it in the first place."

Professor Paradise started looking frantically under bushes. "Out of my way," he said, roughly pushing past Mr Keane, who looked upset.

"Is this a bad time to ask him if he could help give us an idea for our project?" he said.

Sky dragged him away before PP could hit him with a lizard.

"Terrible time," she said.

"I knew this would happen if I let strangers in," said the furious dome owner.

"But, Godpapa," said Sky, "the world is full of strangers."

"I know. That's why I built my own world," he said. "Now go, all of you. OUT! BEGONE!"

And so they were cast out of paradise.

CHAPTER TWENTY

• • • •

Back on the minibus, Mr Keane looked like his old, beaten, miserable self.

"Sorry," he said to Nat, "I thought I was actually going to be able to help for once. Silly me."

He looked out of the window at Sky's little car, disappearing in the distance.

"Winning is so much harder than cheating," said Darius, when Mr Keane had gone.

"I don't like cheating," said Nat.

"So you don't need my evil, sneaky, cheating plan then?" said Darius.

"Shut up, Darius," she said. "This is different. This is an emergency."

Nat looked at Dad. He was sitting next to Dr Nobel, chatting quietly.

"Besides," she added, "these posh kids have got all the advantages. We're cheating to make it fairer."

She didn't QUITE like the sound of that, so she turned to talk to Penny instead.

But Penny said Nat shouldn't cheat so she went off to have dinner with Julia Pryde and Peaches Bleary.

Dad wanted to run a folk-song-writing workshop that night, but someone (Nat) had hidden his ukulele and someone (Nat) had buried his hat so he gave up and went to bed early. He looked a bit sad, and Nat caught Mr Dewdrop putting more Xs on his report.

"Dad makes it very hard for me sometimes," Nat told Penny, as they were tucked up in their sleeping bags. "I have to get ONE night off from him showing me up. That's why I hid the ukulele in the washing-up bowl."

But Penny didn't reply.

Nat tutted and closed her eyes.

She had the strangest dream…

Nat dreamed she was a snuggly, warm, fat

caterpillar. She could feel herself wriggling happily through a cabbage patch. It was so realistic, she could almost taste the lovely soft cabbages. She wriggled for miles, it seemed, feeling the soft breeze on her face and occasionally being tickled by the lovely leaves.

And then she felt herself trying to fly!

It must be time to be a butterfly, she thought.

Then she half-woke in pale sunlight.

It took her a few seconds to realise where she was.

She was in her sleeping bag, but out of her tent.

She was out in the open, and she *was* rising off the ground.

I'm flying – that's nice. Perhaps I am a butterfly, she thought, still befuddled with sleep. *This is great. I'll dive-bomb Darius, that'll scare the little...*

Suddenly she was wide awake.

"YAAAAARGH!" she yelled.

She was dangling, five feet off the ground, from a flipping, flying WEATHER BALLOON that was tied to the hood of her sleeping bag!

"GET ME DOWN!" she screamed, as the breeze took her and wafted her over the yurts.

It must have been Darius, and this was the

absolutely worst thing he'd ever done.

"BAGLEY, YOU MONSTER. I'LL NEVER FORGIVE YOU AND I MEAN IT AND I'M NOT EVEN JOKING!" she yelled.

All the racket started to rouse the entire sleeping camp, and children and teachers alike began staggering out of their tents.

"Somebody help meeee," shouted Nat, floating away.

But everyone was too busy laughing and pointing and fumbling for their cameras to help.

"DAD!" she shouted. "Dad, do something."

"Coming, baby girl," said Dad, in a sleepy panic. He ran out of his tent WITHOUT ANY TROUSERS ON!

"Dad, you're in your pants. Put something on!" yelled Nat.

"No time," said Dad, running after her. "Can you make yourself a bit heavier? You're too high up to reach."

"You're making this worse," shouted Nat, as half-dressed Dad, in bright-white baggy Y-fronts, charged through the camp after his floating daughter.

"Try and go the other way. You're heading for the

field of prize-winning longhorn cows next door and I've been told they're very grumpy – you probably don't want to annoy them," shouted Dad.

It was true: Nat was floating towards the fence.

"How can I go the other way, you moron?" said Nat. "I'm in a balloon, not a jet fighter."

"Yes, OUR weather balloon," shouted Dr Nobel. "That girl's stealing our secret project."

"Don't be ridiculous," said Miss Hunny, wrapping her nightie around her. "She wouldn't even have known it was your secret project. It's just Nathalia and Darius playing again. Our school, um, encourages creative play."

"I have never heard such twaddle in my life," said Dr Nobel. "Your school should be closed down. Your pupils are a menace."

Dad kept jumping up underneath Nat, but she was just too high for him to reach.

"Someone jump on my back!" shouted Dad.

Most children screamed at the thought and dashed back inside their yurts.

"Dolores, help," said Dad, as Miss Hunny ran over to him.

"I'll call the air ambulance," she said. "They'll get

her if she goes too high."

"That's a terrible idea," shouted Nat. "Stop me getting too high."

Then Nat realised she was more worried about *landing* – landing in the field of grumpy cows.

"Dad!" she yelled.

Dad raced for the fence ahead of her. She flew towards his outstretched arms, but then an even bigger gust of wind took her upwards – just out of reach!

Just then a small figure dashed out of nowhere like a blur and jumped on Dad's back, clambering up him until he stood on his head. It was Darius, showing off his chimp-like circus skills.

"I'll get you," he said, grabbing at her.

"Get lost, Bagley," said Nat, kicking out at him through her sleeping bag. "This is all your fault."

"Lift me higher," said Darius, ignoring her.

Dad raised his hands and Darius stood on them.

"OOH," said their audience.

Darius grabbed the bottom of Nat's sleeping bag.

"Why's it so draughty?" said Dad, feeling wind whip around his hairy bare legs.

"What are you wearing, man?" shouted a high-low

voice from the tents. "Or should I say, what AREN'T you wearing?"

"OH HECK," said Dad, suddenly realising he was being stared at IN HIS PANTS by Mr Dewdrop.

"Fudge," said Dad, in a total funk. "Mr Dewdrop won't like this. This isn't what he calls a nice country pursuit. He won't consider my pants professional or becoming."

Quickly Dad covered his shame with his hands.

Unfortunately that meant letting go of Darius, who was left dangling, clinging to the bottom of Nat's sleeping bag.

The two of them sailed gently over the hedge and straight across the field of cows, who were mooing unpleasantly, having been woken up by all the commotion.

"I'm actually going to do you proper, professional-quality harm when I get out of here," said Butterfly Nat.

But now the extra weight was having an effect. They were going down! Just when Nat didn't want them to. The cows looked particularly cross at being disturbed.

"Let go, you total chimp," said Nat. "You're

going to land us both in this field. Sacrifice yourself – get on with it."

"We can make it to the other side," said Darius.

"No we can't," said Nat. "Let go or else."

"If I let go, I'm going to get jabbed."

"Serves you right for tying me to the flipping balloon. Don't deny it. Why on Earth did you do that?"

In her fury she managed to tear a hole in the bottom of her sleeping bag with her foot. She shoved her big toe right up Bagley's squishy little nose.

"Ow. Gerroff!" said Darius.

"I'm gonna rip your nose off, you little monster," said Nat. "Then you'll be even uglier, which is hard to believe."

"Dig your toe in a bit harder – there's a crusty bogey in there that's been stuck for weeks," yelled Darius defiantly.

"AAAAGH," said Nat, disgusted, removing her toe. "You're a maggot, you know that?"

She wiped her wet toe on Darius's short hair.

"Just let go or we're both gonna be cow fodder!" said Nat.

But Darius was determined. He clung on. They

were nearly at the other side of the field.

But the annoyed cows were following them closely, and Nat saw the sharp horns on a prize longhorn called Pointy Doris – she later learned – getting closer to Darius's fat little backside.

"Serves you right," she cackled, as Darius tried frantically to squirm out of the way. "I hope you get jabbed so hard it makes your eyes water."

"No, we can definitely make it," said Darius.
"There's only two metres to go…"

Which was when the balloon popped.

The thin fabric snagged on a spiky tree.

A pointy branch went: *RRRRIIIIIP.*

And the two children plunged downwards.

Nat reached up and grabbed a dangling branch sticking out

from the tree. It held! She hung in the air like a huge wriggling fruit.

Darius wasn't so lucky.

He went straight down.

Straight on to the head of a super-annoyed cow!

Fortunately the sharp horns missed his legs AND his squidgy bits, but it was close enough to make him cross-eyed. He grabbed on to the two horns for dear life as the cow bucked and mooed and tried to throw him off.

"TOTALLY SERVES YOU RIGHT!" yelled Nat from the tree.

With a huge effort, the cow hoisted Darius high into the air and over a hedge.

"NETTLES!" yelled Darius.

"Good," shouted Nat, still dangling.

Two hands grabbed her feet. It was Dad, finally come to the rescue.

She dropped on to his shoulders and he ran for the safety of the fence, ahead of the charging cows.

Dad practically threw Nat over the fence and then hopped over with her. Pointy Doris's head went *BONK* on to the wooden fence, shaking it with a crash.

"Stop frightening my cows," came an angry voice. "They're sensitive creatures and you'll put 'em off they milking."

A fat farmer came puffing up. He ran so fast his cap fell off.

"Oi'll be arsking for compensation from that rotten camp," he said. "All these flipping kids."

He saw Dad get unsteadily to his feet.

"And you should know better, grown man loike you."

"Shut your pie hole," shouted Darius from his nettle bed, in his best Dad impersonation.

The farmer turned to Dad angrily. "What did you say?"

Before Dad could reply, the farmer grabbed a spiky branch.

"Oi've just about had enough of youse lot," he said. "Prepare for a thrashing."

He ran at Dad, waving the branch.

"I'll distract him by running away like I'm scared," said cowardly Dad. "You get back to the camp. RUN."

Everyone ran. The farmer ran after Dad; Nat after Darius.

She didn't care that his face looked all blotchy

from the nettles; she was gonna GET HIM.

Of course, Darius was an evil hiding ninja and Nat trudged back to camp empty-handed.

Rufus was there to greet her.

"That was awesome," he said. "You totally rocked that balloon. I don't care that you've totally ruined our project. You're just WILD."

"You what?" said Nat.

Now she was getting over the shock and panic, she was feeling horribly self-conscious.

She suddenly realised she was still IN HER ONESIE! And it was an old onesie too. With bunnies on.

She felt like she was six, but here she was in the middle of a field, talking to A BOY.

And half the camp WERE WATCHING.

AAAAGH!

"Get lost, go away," she said, running into her yurt and chucking herself on the floor in misery.

Inside, Penny was writing in her diary.

"You're awake early," she said, without looking up.

CHAPTER TWENTY-ONE

••••

THERE WAS A LOT OF FUSS THAT MORNING.
And lots of people were furious.

In no particular order:

Dr Nobel was SO mad. As mad as a baby who'd dropped a dummy down the dunny. His lovely, secret, project-winning weather balloon was in shreds on a tree.

Nat was as mad as Princess Boo in her new single: 'I'm Mad as Heck and It's All Your Fault'. She had SO MANY REASONS TO BE MAD, it would take far too long to list them all.

Dad was as annoyed as someone who'd been chased by an angry farmer. Who, in turn, was as cross as a farmer whose prize-winning cows were being bothered by idiots in balloons.

Mrs Ferret was livid because her camp was turning into a madhouse.

Mr Dewdrop was fuming because the shredded balloon was VERY MESSY.

Mr Bungee was cross because he'd been asleep and missed everything.

Miss Hunny was irritated because her school was looking worse by the day.

Darius wasn't annoyed.

He wandered into Nat's yurt after a while, asking if he'd missed breakfast.

"Oh my God, Darius, you're covered in nettle rash," said Penny. "Or do you shed your skin like a lizard?"

"He actually IS human," said Nat, "although he's going to be an ex-human in a minute."

Darius chucked her sleeping bag at her. "Got it out of a thorn bush."

Nat didn't reply.

"You're covered in thorns," said Penny, fussing over him. She rummaged in her washbag for some first-aid stuff.

"There were some wasps in it," said Darius.

"Oh and you've been STUNG too," said Penny. "Loads of times."

"And an angry badger."

"Are those badger bites? Darius, you poor thing," said Penny. "Well? Nat, say thank you to Darius for rescuing your sleeping bag."

"No thanks," said Nat. "It was his fault it ended up in a thorny bush full of wasps and badgers anyway. It was his fault I got carted off into a tree. It was his fault the whole camp saw me in my bunny onesie."

She was so angry she was almost spitting the words out. "Your stupid plan to win the project competition has gone too far, Bagley. Tying me to a weather balloon was WAY TOO MUCH."

There was silence as Penny rubbed some cream into various red, bumpy and scratched bits.

"Maybe Darius didn't tie you to the balloon," said Penny. "Have you asked him?"

"Of course he did it – he always does it. When have you ever known a time when the answer to 'OMG, who did that, I can't believe someone did that, who in their right mind would do that?' wasn't

'DARIUS BAGLEY DID IT'?"

"Maybe someone else thought they could wreck that school's stupid secret project AND get their own back a teeny bit on someone who's sometimes NOT EVEN THAT NICE TO THEM," said Penny.

"Shut up, Penny," said Nat. "I'm too tired and cross to listen to you babbling on."

"You are IMPOSSIBLE sometimes," snapped Penny, and marched out.

She came back two seconds later to snatch the jar of cream from Darius. She had guessed, correctly, that he was going to eat it.

"What's up with her?" said Nat.

Darius shrugged.

"You can go away too. I'm thinking of evil revenge and I need peace and quiet," she said, climbing into her sleeping bag. "And you can tell everyone I'm not coming out. Ever."

She did finally come out. It took a few hours, but eventually Dad persuaded her, with the help of a crispy, fat, bacon sandwich.

"I need your help," he said.

These were terrifying words, coming from Dad.

"I've been talking to Mr Dewdrop about my chances of getting my certificate," he said.

"Which are?"

"Terrible. He thinks I'm irresponsible."

"You are. Look at me – I dunno how I've survived, Dad, I really don't."

"What would make a big difference is a successful expedition to Bleak Peak."

"Good luck with that."

"Thanks," said Dad, who thought she meant it, "but no one wants to go if I'm coming."

"Are you sure?"

"Some of the children made a poster."

He held it up. It said:

WE'RE NOT GOING TO THE END OF THE FIELD WITH THE GREEN BOGEY, NEVER MIND UP A MOUNTAIN.

"Has everyone signed it?" said Nat.

Dad started reading the names. It took him AGES.

"Not quite everyone," he said.

"Got a pen?" said Nat.

"Be serious," said Dad. "Look, I'd really ever so much appreciate it if you go. How terrible would it look if even my own daughter doesn't trust me?"

"Sorry, too busy staying here plotting Bagley revenge."

"He's coming up the peak," said Dad. "He's the only one who signed up."

Nat thought about this.

On the one hand, Dad was a total menace and didn't know one end of a map from another. Mum said he could get lost going from the bathroom into the kitchen, and she was only half-joking. Dad got lost on his way to school so often, Nat was allowed to turn up late twice a week without getting a pink slip. Mum said his sense of direction was so poor it should be classed as a disability.

On the other hand, Nat pondered, she DID want Dad to get his certificate and get a proper job. Then he'd have to go to work like normal people, and not be able to pop into school "to be helpful" or COME ON CAMP WITH HER EVER AGAIN.

AND if she did go up the peak, there would be plenty of chances to get revenge on Bagley up a lonely mountain.

"OK," she said, "but you know that favour you said you'd do for me?"

"Hmm," said Dad, in that way that meant, '*I MIGHT remember, if you ask for something like an ice cream or a comic, but not if you're going to ask for a pet otter called Susan*'.

"Well, I'd very much like it if you helped us win the geography project on Saturday."

"I'd love to," he said, "but I'm supposed to be neutral, like Mr Bungee. Even though I'm not a teacher, I'm the Green Bogey, remember?"

"Mr Bungee helps the other school all the time," said Nat. "You must have seen him, the big cheaty cheat."

"Why would he do that?" asked Dad.

Nat paused. "You know what, Dad?" she said. "That's a really good question."

CHAPTER TWENTY-TWO

• • • •

JUST AFTER LUNCH, THE BRAVE EXPLORERS TACKLING the trip to the Bleak Peak were assembled and ready to leave.

Darius was there as the bravest of the brave.

Nat was there because Dad made her.

Penny was there because Nat made *her*.

Rufus was there because he wasn't going to let Darius look braver than him.

Plum was there because she was, like: "really, really confident in my own abilities, right, but not big-headed in any way." ("You know those girls who go online to tell you about their Christmas presents and spend five minutes saying how they're honestly not showing off, before spending half an hour MASSIVELY SHOWING OFF?" said Nat to Penny. "That's her, that is.")

Mr Dewdrop was there to mark Dad for his certificate. It really was Dad's last chance; Nat glimpsed Mr D's notebook and Dad had more black Xs than her last biology homework.

Mr Bungee was expedition leader. The first thing he did was snatch the Green Bogey hat off Dad's head.

"This is serious stuff, mate," he said. "No time for being silly."

"I thought you said the Green Bogey WAS serious?" said Dad. "You said he WASN'T a figure of fun but a powerful spirit of the wild."

"And you believed him?" said Rufus, untangling some ropes nearby.

Nat reckoned the posh boy sounded like he didn't care for Mr Bungee much either. *Rufus scores another one*, she thought.

Nat overheard Miss Hunny tell Dad why she DEFINITELY WASN'T COMING, NO FEAR.

"Ivor," she said kindly, cradling a nice hot cup of rosehip tea, "I have been your friend for a long time and I am very fond of you. You have many wonderful qualities."

"I can feel a 'but' coming on," mumbled Dad.

"Yes, you can. Here it is. BUT you have literally no sense of direction, and have NO practical skills. If I had a choice of being stranded in the wilderness with you or a stuffed teddy bear, I'd take the bear. And I'm saying this as a friend."

"Not very friendly," muttered Dad.

"Friends are honest with each other." Miss Hunny smiled. "So, shall I call the emergency services now or wait till it's dark?"

"You're not doing my confidence much good," said Dad, "and I'm a confidence player."

"You'll be totally fine and nothing will happen to you," said Miss Hunny. "Don't forget to pack a lot of emergency flares so people can find your bodies."

"We're only going up a hill. Stop worrying," said Dad, laughing. "And I do wish everyone would stop talking to me like I'm a total spanner."

Dad pottered off, shaking his head.

Miss Hunny beckoned Nat over.

"I got these from camp supplies," said her teacher, handing Nat two cardboard cylinders.

They were heavy in her hands and she read on their sides:

EMERGENCY FLARE. DANGER – CONTAINS EXPLOSIVES.

"Stick these in your backpack," said Miss Hunny. "Don't look so alarmed, Nathalia, it's just in case. Oh and for heaven's sake, don't show them to Darius. He's not the best reader in the world but somehow even he can recognise the word 'explosive'."

"I think he can smell it, Miss," said Nat. "He's got a very good sense of smell, like a lot of wild creatures."

"You really are the strangest class I've ever taught," said Miss Hunny. "And please tell me why Penny Posnitch is walking around holding a stick."

"She bet Darius fifty pence she could find underground water," said Nat heavily.

"I wonder if St Scrofula's needs a new English teacher," said Miss Hunny quietly.

"Maybe. Their last one just wrote a bestseller," said Nat.

"I hate that school," muttered Miss Hunny. She drained her cup of rosehip. "And unless you lot come up with a brilliant project in the next couple of days, they're going to make us look like... like the losers we are."

Nat was startled. Miss Hunny never got cross but she sounded properly annoyed now.

"Sorry," said her form teacher. "Forget I said anything. Have fun... and don't forget the flares."

None of the St Scrofula's teachers was going on the trip. Since the destruction of their swanky weather balloon, they'd been working flat out with plans for a brand-new project for the competition.

Nat could see them all, excitedly huddled around in a field, as she grabbed her backpack. They had pens and papers and laptops and maps and compasses and it was clear they had A NEW AND EVEN MORE AWESOME PROJECT.

Her classmates and teachers were taking this exciting opportunity to... catch some rays and chat. Miss Austen and Miss Eyre were playing cards on a log. Miss Hunny was reading a story to tough guy Marcus Milligan, who was missing his mum. Flora Marling sat on a swing hanging from an oak, fans at her feet, hair golden in the afternoon sunlight. She looked up and smiled at Nat. It was a vision of heaven.

Darius let one off.

"Better out than in," he said, jumping on the minibus.

"You not joining in the boffin-fest?" Nat asked Rufus, as they boarded the minibus. She pointed to his classmates, working away.

The boy shook his head. "You don't know how lucky you are, not having to win all the time."

I wouldn't mind winning ONCE though, thought Nat. *Once would be nice.*

Mr Bungee insisted on driving. He was one of those blokes who drove with his arm out of the window, radio on full blast, foot hard down on the accelerator pedal. He cut up all the other, smaller cars on the road, refused to pull over in narrow places, and was generally a total road hog.

Nat, being bounced about in the back, thought his driving was even worse than Dad's – although this minibus didn't break down and there wasn't a line of angry motorists stuck behind him, honking horns and shouting rude words.

An hour later, Mr Bungee screeched to a halt in a gravel car park, just off a small road. There was a dirt path into a small wood and a big green sign nearby which read:

BLEAK PEAK COUNTRY PARK

Underneath was another sign. That one said:

KEEP IT NICE! NO DOGS, NO PICNICS, NO TODDLERS, NO RADIOS, NO BIKES, NO SKATEBOARDS, NO ICE CREAM/BURGER/KEBAB VANS, NO RUNNING, NO SWIMMING, NO SINGING, NO BALL GAMES, NO GUNS, NO KNIVES, NO AEROSOLS, NO HORSE RIDING, NO BOTTLES, NO CANS, NO ROLLERBLADES, NO FEEDING THE BIRDS, NO HUNTING, NO FISHING. NO CLAPPING, NO CHEERING, NO ARGUING.

Underneath some wit had scrawled:

No fun, no point, go home.

"WE put that sign up," said Mr Dewdrop proudly. "I think we covered everything."

"Does it say anything about farting?" said Darius. "Cos I am brewing."

"I'll make a note," said Mr Dewdrop darkly.

"Let's start," said Mr Bungee, when everyone was far enough away from Darius to concentrate. He took a great big map out.

"Don't you know the way?" asked Dad.

He hadn't meant to be sarcastic, but Mr Bungee

seemed offended.

"Why don't you show us?" said the New Zealander.

"Great," said Dad, sidling up, "I need to prove I know what I'm doing." He indicated Mr Dewdrop.

Mr B gave Dad a smile. Nat thought it looked as friendly as a fox in a henhouse.

"Fill your boots," said Mr B, handing Dad the map and a huge, complicated compass. "You know how to work this, I suppose?"

"Are left and right marked on it?" said Dad.

Nat groaned.

Mr Bungee grinned. "Still joking, I see. Nice. But no more jokes till we make camp, OK? It looks pretty tame now but there's a fog from the sea that can cover the mountain in minutes, trust me."

"Fog. Right," said Dad, staring at the compass.

Mr B pointed a few things out. "The scale is there, the index line's there, and the orientation lines are *there*. It's pretty standard."

"Got you," said Dad, sounding alarmed.

"Now, look on this Ordnance Survey map," said Mr Bungee, grabbing the massive map that crinkled and flapped in the wind. "We need to reach the disused mine first, then take our bearings from there."

"Erm…" said Dad. "I think it's that way." He confidently pointed… back at the minibus. "Only kidding," he said, turning and pointing into the woods.

Mr Bungee looked at Dad carefully. "I think we should be a bit more accurate, eh?"

Darius came over and looked at the map, frowning.

Mr Bungee impatiently pushed him out of the way with the side of his boot.

"We're here," said Mr Bungee. "Let's see. Hmm. First, find our easting… So that's 26–5, yes?"

"That's right," said Dad. "Well done."

"Ah, then northings. Would you say that's 45–8?"

"Well, more or less," said Dad confidently.

"Add the prefix so that's SQ. 26–5, 45–8. And we need to get to…?"

There was a horrible pause.

Nat died a little inside. Dad saw her expression and a determined look spread on his face.

He made a decision, shoved the map in his backpack and strode off into the woods.

"Follow me," he said. "It's all in my brain now."

But you haven't got a brain, thought Nat, trudging behind. *We're doooomed.*

CHAPTER TWENTY-THREE

••••

But they weren't doooomed immediately. It took hours.

"We'll just stay on the path," declared Dad, striding ahead confidently. "It's going upwards, which is good."

"Don't you want to take the shortcut by the farm at grid reference 25–5, 35–8?" said Mr Bungee.

"Terrible idea," said Dad, loud enough for Mr Dewdrop to hear. "There's all sorts of hidden dangers that I can see, being the experienced guide that I am. No point risking it with kids, is what I say. Let's stick to the nice safe path."

Nat still wasn't talking to Darius, and Penny was

being a bit off with her for some stupid reason, so she found herself walking in step with Rufus.

"Does your dad actually know what he's doing?" he asked.

"That's not really how my dad works," she said, with a sigh.

They walked in silence for a while. The forest thinned out and the ground became steeper and rockier.

"Sorry about your weather balloon," said Nat eventually. "Have you got another project for Saturday?"

"Dunno if I should tell you," Rufus said.

Nat's heart lurched. *Has he guessed I'm a double agent?*

"Why's that?" she squeaked, trying to sound innocent but actually sounding GUILTY AS CHARGED.

"Because I've got a horrible feeling we're cheating and I'm a bit embarrassed about it."

OMG, thought Nat, *I've got away with it. Tee-hee.*

"If I tell you, you mustn't tell anyone," he said. "Promise?"

Nat was stuck. She needed to know, but she HAD NEVER EVER BROKEN A PROMISE.

She could admit that sometimes she was cheaty, grumpy, sneaky, pinchy, fibby, and probably a couple more too (*I sound like the evil seven dwarves*, she thought to herself), but she'd never broken a promise. And she wasn't going to start now.

"Promise," she said.

But before he could tell her, they had reached the top of a ridge and come to the foothills of the peak. The view took their breath away.

The hillside was, as the name suggested, bleak. It felt like they were miles from anywhere. All around them lay purple heather, grey rocks, and dark-green scrub. It was wild and, Nat had to admit, quite lovely. In front of them skittered a wide, fast-flowing stream.

For the first time in a week, she felt a kind of peace.

It lasted one-and-a-half seconds.

Not bad going for me, she reckoned.

"This is all wrong," shouted Mr Bungee, stomping to the front of the group. "I reckon we're a mile from the old mine."

"We just need to follow that stream upwards," said Dad, who had just sneaked a peek at the map and could at least recognise a stream.

"It's DOWNSTREAM, dummy," said Mr Bungee. "You're a bit of a menace with maps, mate."

He grabbed the map from Dad's rucksack.

"Bit rude," said Dad.

Nat got worried. Dad was ever so mild-mannered, but he hated rudeness. And the only things he hated more than rudeness were PEOPLE IN AUTHORITY.

"I'm in charge," yelled Mr Bungee, "and don't you forget it."

Uh-oh, thought Nat.

Dad's normally happy face darkened.

"HE's been helping us cheat," whispered Rufus, indicating Mr Bungee. "He's sucking up cos he wants a job teaching PE at our school. How awful would that be?"

Nat's suspicions were correct! He *was* helping St rotten cheaty Scrofula's. She felt a bit better about her cheating now.

She *had* to tell Darius! But how?

"I heard everything, ha!" said ninja Darius,

appearing behind them like a ragged ghost.

"EEEK! Stop doing that!" yelled Nat.

"You mustn't tell anyone," said Rufus, panicking.

"Nat might have promised, but I didn't," said Darius, dashing into the scrub and hiding. "Well done, Buttface," he yelled.

Rufus turned to her angrily. "Oh, I see your game," he said. "Very clever, I must say."

Desperately, Nat called to Penny, "Tell Rufus I'm not a horrible spanner."

"Sometimes you're a horrible spanner," shouted Penny.

"She doesn't mean it," said Nat. "It's lack of oxygen in her brain with all the walking."

Rufus stomped off.

Plum looked at Nat and treated her to a sickly smile. "Still making friends, I see," she said.

"You're going in that stream," said Nat, seeing the red mist again and running at her.

"AAAAH!" shouted Plum, dashing into trees for cover.

Over by the stream, Mr Bungee and Dad were now wrestling with the map. Penny had thrown herself on the ground in misery. Rufus was swishing a big stick in the heather, trying to poke out Darius, who was telling him he couldn't catch him in a properly rude way. And Plum was shrieking that she was going to be streamed to death. It was chaos.

Mr Dewdrop dropped his clipboard in dismay. "Oh my," he said, "this competition was the worst idea ever. The countryside is for nice people, not YOU LOT!"

"Gimme that map, Bumolé," said Mr Bungee.

"Ask me nicely," said Dad. "I'm not very good at taking orders. I have to warn you, I can get very cross."

"You?" said Mr Bungee, snatching the map. "You couldn't get cross if your life depended on it. You're a puny Pom who's never had to do a proper day's work in his life."

"Oh yeah?" said Dad. "Comedy-writing is flipping hard work. It's like being down a coal mine, only I'm digging pure comedy, not lumps of coal, and I haven't even got a drill. Or a canary."

"Canary?"

"Yeah, to see if there's gas," said Dad. "But we're getting off the point."

"Look at my muscles," said Mr Bungee. "*This* is

what a man looks like." He took off his shirt and chucked it on the ground.

Nat had to admit, he did have muscles.

Dad started to take off his shirt too.

"NOOOOO!" shouted Nat, hiding her face in her hands.

Dad took a good look at Mr Bungee's rippling chest and thick bulging arms and hard stomach, and quickly buttoned his shirt back up.

He took a step towards Mr Bungee. "I'm an imaginative person. My muscles are all in my imagination," he said.

Nat groaned. She didn't think Dad meant it like that.

Mr Bungee roared sarcastically. He waved the map in Dad's face.

"Don't do that," said Dad.

"What you gonna do about it, Green Bogey Man?" said Mr Bungee. "Write a song? Make a funny joke?" He jabbed Dad with the map again.

"I'm warning you," said Dad.

"This is usually when you run away," shouted Nat, which was true but not very helpful.

But Dad wasn't running. He was CROSS.

Then Nat saw Mr Bungee draw a big, meaty fist back. With utter horror, she realised he was going to HIT DAD.

Everything went in slow motion.

Dad also realised he was going to be thumped and started to dodge.

Mr Bungee dropped the map, but the wind blew it into his face, blocking his vision.

Darius somehow appeared right in front of Mr Bungee, making rude faces at Rufus, who was CHARGING AT HIM WITH A BIG STICK.

"Aaaagh!" shouted Dad, about to be walloped.

"AAAAGH!" shouted Rufus, charging like a wild beast.

"TOO RUDE TO PRINT," shouted Darius at the boy.

DODGE, went Darius, at the crucial moment.

WHOMP! went the stick in Mr Bungee's tenders.

"*HHHHHHNNNNNGGGGG*," went Mr B, and folded up like one of Dad's DIY projects.

SPLASH! went the big man, right into the stream.

"You saw that!" he screamed at Mr Dewdrop, who hadn't been looking because he was too busy writing on his clipboard. "You saw what he… glub,

glub… did!"

Darius grabbed the stick off Rufus and quickly chucked it out of sight.

Mr Bungee went skidding off downstream, shouting threats and all sorts of other things.

There was a horrid silence.

Dad looked around him.

"That's settled then," he said cheerfully. "Upstream it is."

CHAPTER TWENTY-FOUR

• • • •

AS THEY WALKED ON, FOLLOWING THE STREAM, Nat had a horrible feeling that somewhere, somehow, she'd been the cause of all the trouble.

She watched Mr Dewdrop glaring at Dad as they trudged up the peak and wondered if he'd ever get his certificate now.

She looked at Rufus and Plum. If she DID get sent to that school, she'd already made two enemies. Before she'd even started.

Then she looked at Penny's sulky face and thought she wasn't doing brilliantly with her friends at her own school, either.

At least I've still got my pet goblin, she thought,

as Darius burped the new Adele single behind her.

Then she remembered the weather-balloon/ bunny-onesie humiliation and thought he wasn't a very TAME pet goblin.

Then, within five minutes, they were walking in mist. And then cloud. And soon they were wet with water droplets and shrouded in fog.

"It's a bit dangerous up here. We need to make for the rangers' hut and wait until the fog lifts," said Mr Dewdrop. "Mr Bumolé, it's all in your head, eh? Let's hope so."

"No worries," said Dad, sounding INCREDIBLY WORRIED.

Darius darted forward, out of Nat's sight.

"Where are you off to?" she called, but there was no answer.

"This fog is shocking," said Rufus. "I can't see a thing."

"I'm scared," said super-confident Plum.

"All stay together," said Dad, noticing the sound of fear in the children and taking charge. "Single file now, and make sure there's someone in front of you at all times. Mr Dewdrop, you stay at the rear."

"I know we're not actually far away from the

town," said Nat, after they had trudged for what seemed like ages, "but it feels like a million miles."

"My divining stick tells me we're on the crossroads of two ley lines," said Penny. The fog muffled her voice. It was spooky.

Nat shivered, although she didn't believe in such rubbish.

"Stop going on about ley lines," snapped Nat. "You sound like a spanner."

"If you get cross on a ley line, terrible things happen," said Penny. "You can believe it or not, but it's true."

"Terrible things happen to me all the time," said Nat.

The fog was really thick now.

"Everyone stay together," yelled Dad. "Someone sing!"

Darius started singing…

He started singing verse 657 of his endless, epic poem "Diarrhoea".

"There's a squelching in your shoe and it's something very new; dia — "

"Do *not* sing that!" yelled Mr Dewdrop, who felt sick.

Darius tried again…

"My love is like a red red rose,

She's deeply in my heart…"

"Aah, that's better," said Mr Dewdrop. Nat just giggled.

"But even deeper in my tum

"I've brewed a massive—"

"No, it's worse," yelled Dad.

"Sing a nice song," said Mr Dewdrop. "Something by Coldplay maybe."

"No," said Dad, "we need to cheer them up. What's that new song that everyone likes? You know, that girl who won the singing competition. Annie Pleasant."

Dad didn't know that Annie Pleasant had recently had a makeover. She was now called Crazy Annie.

So Darius treated them to the latest hit single from DJ Naughty versus Crazy Annie, "What Makes My Booty Bounce".

It wasn't rude until the second verse.

Then it was SO, SO RUDE. It appeared that rather a large number of things made her booty bounce.

"Stop it at once," said Mr Dewdrop, sounding

shocked. "There's a law against that sort of thing here."

But all the kids knew the song and now they all joined in on the chorus.

Darius was well ahead, and everyone jogged to keep up with his 'PG-rated' voice.

"Mr Bumolé, is this your idea of an appropriate song?" said Mr Dewdrop angrily

"I think that's as rude as it gets," said Dad hopefully.

He'd forgotten about the rap in the middle. Darius had not.

Dad started coughing to cover up the loud, rude words. But there were so many.

"I wanna **COUGH** and **COUGH** with a **COUGH**, **COUGH**, **COUGH**, and then I'm gonna **COUGH**, **COUGH** bounce my **COUGH** and then **COUGH** hot **COUGH**, **COUGH** stiggity **COUGH**."

Dad was running out of breath. Unlike Darius, who could happily go on for *days*.

"**WHEEEZE**, you're my swag bag, **WHEEZE**, **SPLUTTER**, lime Jell-O, **SHUT UP, DARIUS···** you say 'yo' baby I say 'whut?' **YES!** talk to my hand or … **HUT! I FOUND THE HUT! STOP SINGING – WE'RE SAFE!**" yelled Dad with the last of his breath.

He had made a grab for Darius but somehow, miraculously, found the rangers' hut instead! He grasped the handle, yanked it open – and fell in.

Everyone else piled in, trampling over him as they went.

"That's fine," said trampled Dad, "don't worry about me, glad to help. Mr Dewdrop, please put that in your notebook rather than the song."

He struggled to his feet and looked around the hut. "Night will be coming on soon," he said decisively. "I think we should stay here until the morning. I don't want to take any risks."

Nat looked at her father. Every once in a while she wondered if he was really as useless and hopeless as he always appeared. Then he tripped over a bit of rope and fell into a cupboard full of tins of soup.

They investigated the hut. It was filled with bunk beds and warm woollen blankets. There was a stove and a cupboard full of supplies, including dented soup tins. They could last a month in a zombie apocalypse, never mind a foggy night.

"Are we all here?" said Mr Dewdrop, doing a quick head count. "Well done, Mr Bumolé, for finding this hut in the fog," he said, rubbing out the

X he'd just put in his notebook.

"Actually, I think Darius found it," whispered Nat to Penny.

She remembered Darius at the riverbank, studying the map. Of course! Everyone at school thought Darius was one step removed from a dunce, but Nat knew he was just *different*.

An unexpected but annoying wave of affection for him washed over her.

Darius took his muddy boots off and gnawed his toenails, like a baboon. He spat out the bits into the back of Plum's hair.

Nat smiled.

Yes, he was VERY different.

Dad quickly got the stove alight, only burning his eyebrows once, and started happily frying things out of tins.

Soon the little hut was warm and cheerful. And after they had eaten, everyone felt better.

Penny started telling spooky ghost stories. She was brilliant at it. Nat suspected that, as far as Penny was concerned, these weren't stories – this was NEWS.

Nat was starting to feel a bit less furious with

Darius and slid up to him on a bunk.

"Listen, chimpy," she said. "I know I told you to come up with an evil plan, but you went too far with the whole tying-me-to-a-weather-balloon thing."

Nat didn't expect an apology, because Darius never apologised. And she didn't really mind too much, because she knew he was never sorry.

But what happened next totally threw her.

There was a very, very long silence.

Eventually, he spoke.

"It wasn't me," said Darius simply.

Nat could not speak. She was actually shocked. Darius hadn't shocked her since about week two at school; she was totally used to him. BUT HE'D NEVER EVER LIED TO HER BEFORE.

She was genuinely hurt. She was too hurt to pinch him or make him eat grass or do Chinese burns or carry out any of the other thousand things she did to him on a daily basis.

She was more hurt by this lie than the balloon trick itself.

She looked around the hut. Everyone seemed to be getting on – even Mr Dewdrop was laughing – and she suddenly felt homesick and friendless and alone and miserable.

"I'm going out," she said, taking her backpack. "I may be some time."

She left the hut, but no one had noticed.

Typical, she thought, sitting on a big rock and looking up at the stars. *Nobody cares.*

Her backpack lay at her feet. She opened the top. There were the emergency flares.

I feel like letting one off, she thought, *then everyone would be sorry.*

She picked up a flare.

"What are you doing out here?" said Penny, who'd followed her into the night.

"Penny, everything's terrible," said Nat, "but you wouldn't understand."

"Try me," said Penny coldly.

"Haven't you been here this week?" said Nat. "Haven't you seen what I've gone through?"

"Actually," said Penny, "I've heard a lot of people say they've had a nice time."

"They're not me," grumbled Nat. "And now the ONE person I can rely on has LIED TO ME."

"The one person?" shouted Penny. "You think Darius is the only person you can rely on? That's two stupid things you've said right there. One is that he's the ONLY person. And the other is that you can't rely on Darius – are you mad?"

"He's never lied to me before," said Nat, "but now he's telling me he didn't tie me to the balloon."

"He didn't, you moron," said Penny. "BECAUSE I DID!"

Nat was so shocked she jumped.

AND PULLED THE CORD.

AND SET OFF THE FLARE!

The flare burst out of the tube like a rocket – because it was a rocket. Blazing red smoke poured out as it arced high into the night sky. It exploded, becoming a dazzling cloud. It lit up a massive area.

It could be seen from space, thought Nat. *That's not good.*

But first there was something to deal with right here on Earth.

"YOU?" said Nat. "Why?"

"Because you've been a total meanie since we got here."

"Give me one example."

"You said I thought I was a fairy princess from the cloud city of la-la land."

"Give me another example."

"You spend all your time trying to suck up to other girls, and take me for granted."

"Stop giving me examples."

But Penny didn't. She listed Nat's crimes, ending with:

"And you haven't done anything to help us with the competition except try to spoil the other school's project."

"YOU burst their secret balloon," said Nat.

"OK, that was a bad example," said Penny, looking guilty, "but you made me do it."

"You're supposed to be my friend."

"I am. I'm a friend to the real Nathalia, the one who's helpful and thoughtful and kind and makes everyone laugh."

"They laugh AT me, Penny."

"Sometimes AT, sometimes WITH," admitted Penny. "But, anyway, your real friends are me and Darius, and you never think about us."

"Not true," gasped Nat.

"'Tis true. In all your worrying about changing schools, you've only thought about yourself. You've never once thought that Darius and I might MISS YOU."

Penny turned on her heel and went back indoors.

Her words clanged in Nat's brain, like a clapper in a big brass bell.

Oh pooh, thought Nat, and waited for the emergency rescue team.

I certainly need rescuing, she thought, as the first blue lights appeared, *but I don't think this lot can help*.

CHAPTER TWENTY-FIVE

••••

THE NEXT FEW HOURS WHIZZED PAST IN AN embarrassing sort of blur.

Bits of it stuck out as particularly wretched for Nat though:

There was the look on Dad's face when he saw she'd let off a distress flare.

There was the look on Mr Dewdrop's face as he shouted at Dad for letting her come up here CARRYING DANGEROUS EXPLOSIVES.

There was the look on the rescue rangers' faces when they realised they'd rangered all this way up the flipping peak for a rescue and NO ONE NEEDED RESCUING.

The same went for the air ambulance crew.

"We might send you a bill for this," said the grumpy pilot.

"Can I have a ride in your chopper?" said Darius.

"Ooh, I never knew air ambulance pilots knew words like that," said Mr Dewdrop, still shocked at something they'd said to him.

And of course Mr Bungee turned up.

He said he was here to help, but Nat thought he'd come to gloat.

Mr Bungee insisted on taking them all back to camp.

By the time the adventurers returned, the whole camp knew about their woeful adventure, so there was a lot of midnight sniggering to deal with.

Miss Hunny didn't snigger. She hugged Nat because she'd been so worried. It was soppy Miss H who had called the air ambulance out when she listened in to the rescue rangers' radio.

"I knew I shouldn't have let you go," she said to Dad. "You're a total liability."

"I AGREE!" shouted Mr Dewdrop, and handed Dad a certificate with the words **TOTALLY FAILED** across it in big letters.

Dad wasn't even cross with Nat, which made her feel even more wretched.

"I deserve a telling-off," she said to Darius, as he wandered off to his chalet.

"Yeah, you do," he said.

"I feel totally rotten."

"You probably do."

"I think I've got everything wrong this week."

"Yup."

"And I've just had another horrid thought: I've only got a day to put our project together for the competition and I haven't done a thing."

"Shame."

"And I've spent so long worrying about myself that I haven't realised I'm going to let my whole class down. And I actually *care* about my class."

"Hmm. Night then."

"NOT TELLING ME OFF IS MAKING ME FEEL WORSE!" she shouted.

"Oh dear," said Darius with a grin, and slammed the door.

Nat went back to an empty yurt. Penny was so upset she insisted on sleeping in Miss Hunny's tent.

It was a long, cold, lonely night for Nat.

The next morning, Dad woke her early and drove her into town.

They didn't say much on the way, except for Dad apologising to her! Which made her feel way worse.

"You must have been feeling pretty rotten to send the emergency signal," he said. "Sorry I wasn't looking after you better."

"Dad…" began Nat, but she couldn't finish.

"I'm just glad you're OK," he said. "When I heard the rescue rangers, I thought my heart would stop."

Could I feel worse? thought Nat.

Then Dad pulled up at a little B&B and Mum was there waiting – and, yes, Nat FELT WORSE.

Mum gave her a big hug and things seemed better.

"Where's my poor, little, rescued grandchild?" said Bad News Nan, sitting wedged in at the breakfast table.

"Nan!" shouted Nat, surprised.

"I thought I'd stay a few days," said Bad News Nan. "They do lovely breakfasts here, as much as you can eat, and it's included in the price."

"We're going bankrupt," muttered the owner of

the B&B, bringing Nan more sausages.

"I took a few days off when your dad called last night," said Mum, after Nat had forced down porridge, bacon, eggs, beans, hash browns and toast, and was eyeing up a bit of fruit cake on the sideboard. "Thought I'd see what was going on."

Nat explained that she basically felt like an utter spanner. "And it's not even totally all entirely Dad's fault," she said.

"I bet he helped," said Mum gently, and they all laughed.

Nat groaned. "AND by tomorrow I'm supposed to put together a big project on what we've learned on this week's field trip. But all I've learned is that sometimes I can be a teeny-tiny bit self-centred. Sometimes. Does anyone want that last bit of toast?"

"Come on, love," said Dad. "You've also learned how to ride a horse backwards, how to dangle upside down from trees, not to look into a volcano, how to flash your pants, and the best way to fly a weather balloon."

Mum looked at Dad sternly. "Tell me you've made that up," she said.

"Erm…" said Dad.

Just then, Mr Keane arrived with Sky.

"We wanted to see if you're OK," he said, pulling up a couple of chairs.

"I'm not going back," Nat said. "Everybody hates me. My classmates have had a rotten time and blame me for it. The posh kids hate me cos I've been super sneaky. And my friends hate me because I've been ever such a little bit horrible."

"We thought you might say that," said Mr Keane. "So look outside."

Nat looked out of the window. "AAAGH! It's a lynch mob!" she said dramatically. "Hide me."

"Don't be silly," said Mum, looking out of the window and understanding. "Off you go, dear, head held high."

Nat walked out into the garden of the B&B. There, standing in front of the minibus, were Rufus, Plum, Penny, Darius, Milly Barnacle, Julia Pryde AND... AND FLORA MARLING!

Flora ran over and GAVE HER A HUG.

"Wurble?" said Nat, confused.

"When we heard the rescue people were called, we were worried sick," said Flora.

"It's true," said Julia Pryde. "We do sort of like

you, you know. We didn't want anything to actually happen to you."

"Also, without you around, one of us would end up with Darius," said Milly Barnacle, with a shudder.

Darius glared at her.

Penny grabbed Nat's hand. "Friends stick together," she said. "Even slightly rubbish friends."

Nat squeezed her hand.

"And we know why you've been trying so hard to beat us," said Rufus. "It's this stupid competition."

"We're sick of competitions," said Plum. "Everything we do at school is a competition too."

"It's that rotten Mr Dewdrop's fault," said Flora.

"Him and that Mr Bungee," said Rufus, "stirring things up."

"I wish there was a way to get them," said Penny.

"Like a really evil, sneaky way?" said Nat.

Everyone looked at Darius.

Eventually, they all headed back to the camp.

Mum had said she was going to come to the school's big project displays tomorrow. That made Nat feel really happy AND really nervous at the same time. Which was kind of the effect Mum had on a lot of people, Nat reckoned.

But things weren't looking good for Dad, the big idiot.

As soon as they got back, Dad was summoned to the camp office. Nat heard Mr Dewdrop threatening some kind of investigation.

Darius was sent to listen at the door of the meeting. When he came back, he looked grave.

"Something about pressing charges," said Darius. "They've got the park rangers, the Ferret woman, Mr Bungee and even the local police involved. I don't think it's going brilliantly."

Nat had been feeling really cheerful. Now she crashed down to Earth.

ALL MY FAULT, she kept thinking.

She wandered off on her own and watched the grumpy cows for a bit.

Suddenly, she was aware of Sky standing next to her.

"You've been ever so lovely," said Nat, "and I don't actually even know your full name."

Sky coughed. "I didn't tell you," she said. "It's Brown."

"Brown?" said Nat. "Sky *Brown*?"

"I don't think my parents thought it through

properly," said Sky. "They just liked the name Sky."

"Well, my name's even more awful," said Nat. "Bumolé. Dad says it's posh French and is pronounced Bew-mow-lay, but we're not in posh France, are we? We're here and here everyone here says Bumhole. Or worse."

"Whoa. Parents are lame," said Sky.

"Totally," said Nat, trying to sound like the older woman.

"Could be worse," said Sky coolly. "There's a tribe I know that feed their kids to crocodiles."

"That's terrible parenting," said Nat, trying to sound as cool as Sky.

"Yeah," said Sky.

"My dad once projected my naked baby photos on to the wall at a school disco," said Nat.

"Impressive," said Sky.

"And he comes into the girls' changing rooms in Topshop to help with my buttons."

"Cringe," said Sky sympathetically.

"And he hasn't got a real job – he writes the jokes in Christmas crackers."

"Ouch."

"And he's always at my school, and he plays the

ukulele in public, and he tries to do DIY and gets it wrong and blows a lot of things up."

Sky was laughing now.

Nat couldn't help it; she joined in.

"Once," she said, "he sank a fleet of super-expensive boats and he electrocuted some priceless ducks AND he got us thrown into proper jail and I'm not even joking."

"That's pretty bad," giggled Sky.

"Not as bad as the crocodiles though," said Nat, "if I'm being honest."

There was a pause.

"I miss my dad," said Sky. "He was a total spanner too. He used to organise loads of stuff for this town. He ran the boating lake. He planned all the carnivals, and organised a big bonfire and the summer fête. He was at the front of every parade, wearing a silly hat, blowing a trumpet out of tune."

Nat gently placed her hand on Sky's shoulder.

"He raised loads for charity – he was one of those dads who's always in a funny costume. He was the one wearing a nappy in the local marathon, and he was always the back end of the donkey in the local panto. Practically every time I saw him he was in fancy dress. Honestly, he totally used to make me squirm!"

Sky took a deep breath.

"When he died, the life seemed to go out of the town, you know? It isn't the same without him. I never thought I'd miss being embarrassed, but I do, almost every day."

Nat felt a lump in her throat, but Sky just squeezed her hand and smiled.

"That's when I started travelling. Maybe I've been looking for something to replace him with, but I haven't found it yet."

To her horror, Nat found herself on the verge of blubbing.

"I love my dad and I've ruined his life," she wailed. "If anything ever happens to him, I'll have to travel up the Limpopo river and climb mountains to try and find something too, but I'm not a very good swimmer and I don't like heights and I don't want my bits getting munched off by sharks either. I just want to stay at school and do my GCSEs."

Sky wrapped her arms round Nat. "Don't be silly," she said, "I'm sure you haven't ruined his life. Have you?"

Nat's lower lip trembled. "Possibly," she said.

"Well, we'll just have to *un*-ruin it then," Sky said firmly.

CHAPTER TWENTY-SIX

• • • •

THAT FRIDAY WAS ONE OF THE BUSIEST DAYS the Lower Snotley Eco Camp could remember. Because it was a day of PLANS. EVERYONE was making them.

Except Dad. Dad was marched off the site and forbidden from coming back. He told Nat he'd see her tomorrow and gave Darius his Green Bogey hat.

"Wear it with pride," said Dad, with dignity.

Some of the plans being hatched were heart-warming and uplifting and lovely; others were dark and devious.

And it was very hard to untangle which plans were which.

Children and teachers alike spent the morning dashing from classroom to classroom and from yurt to yurt, with bits of paper, photos, laptops, rocks, soil samples, measurements, and equipment.

Arguments, discussions and the occasional scuffle broke out.

Mysteriously, several teachers and at least half of the children then disappeared for the rest of the day.

A day in which muffled explosions could be heard all along the coast.

The group only came back late that night, filthy and exhausted. But triumphant.

Ready for tomorrow.

Carnival day.

Project day.

Competition day.

D-DAY.

Nat was wide awake just after dawn. She slipped past the snoring Penny and rapped on the door of Darius's hut.

He was wide awake too.

"Ready?" she said.

"Ready," he said.

"Ready," said Rufus behind her.

"Ready," said Mr Keane, behind him.

"I wasn't ready," said Penny sleepily. "What day is it?"

At 10am sharp, the children from both schools, plus their teachers, were taken into Lower Snotley to present their competition projects in the Nice 'N' Neat Alliance offices.

It might have been Nat's imagination, but she reckoned the people of the little town looked a little livelier today. There were smiles on their faces. They waved at the children happily.

And was that someone taking the chains off the boating-lake swans?

"They're beginning to look a bit less like zombies around here," she said to Darius.

Mr Dewdrop and his equally neat colleagues were fussing around in the hall, not doing very much except getting in the way.

Both schools had mysterious crates with them, and they were given an hour to set out their projects before Mr Bungee and Mrs Ferret, the mayor, the local paper, and various town bigwigs arrived.

"No entry till we're ready," said Miss Hunny, waving Mr Dewdrop away and out of the hall.

"That's right," said Dr Nobel. "There's very special equipment here – very delicate – and you might disturb it."

"Oh no, you're quite right. There's been enough disturbance around here already," said Mr Dewdrop, scurrying off.

There was just enough time to get everything ready.

The doors opened.

It wasn't only the Lower Totley great and good who came.

At 11am, the hall started filling up with locals. The Heads of both schools arrived shortly afterwards. Nat's Head turned up in a tatty old banger; the Head of St Scrofula's, Dame Nellie Fishstick, in the school's helicopter.

"I know it looks flash," she said to Nat's Head, as they walked in together, "but I need to be at a function two hundred miles away this afternoon."

"You on the run?" said Darius, hurrying past with a jug of orange juice.

"Hilarious," said Dame Nellie, taking a seat.

"Who does the goblin belong to?"

Nat's Head grabbed her as she hurried past. "I've heard some very odd reports this week," she said. "How many are true?"

"All of them, I should think, Miss," said Nat.

"Hmm, I see. Now, how many can we deny and how many can we get away with?"

Fortunately, Nat didn't have to answer because the hall doors were flung open and in strode... Professor Paradise. He sat on a chair marked: **GUEST OF HONOUR**.

Nat looked at him in alarm, but he just smiled at her.

Mum and Dad both arrived, ignoring Mr Bungee and Mrs Ferret, who took places on the judging platform, along with Mr Dewdrop.

Mum called over to Nat, "Nan sends her love, but they've got black pudding on the menu this morning so she might be some time. She does like her black pudding."

Finally, the hip-hop-loving old lady Nat had met earlier in the week showed up. Without her scarf, but wearing a MAYORAL CHAIN!

NOTHING IS EVER WHAT IT SEEMS,

thought Nat loudly in her head.

"Hello, dear," said the mayor. "I have a feeling this day is going to be remembered for a very long time."

When everyone was in, Mr Dewdrop looked at his watch, tutted because they were one minute late, and said a few dreary words about the competition – and a lot of even drearier words about how great the Nice 'N' Neat Countryside Alliance was and how much they'd improved the town since moving their HQ here.

A grumble from the audience told Nat a different story, but she was feeling too nervous about her presentation to think about it too long.

Because now it was HER TURN!

She stood up and began, looking at Mr Keane for support. He smiled.

Then she looked at Dr Nobel. He smiled too.

Then Rufus walked up and stood by Nat.

"One at a time," shouted Mr Dewdrop, but the children ignored him.

"We'd like to show you a short film of our week here," said Nat and Rufus together.

The lights dimmed and Darius began the video.

It was made from loads of mobile-phone footage and photos. The video featured children from both schools working together and HAVING FUN.

The video had been skilfully edited to avoid some of Nat's *most* embarrassing escapades, although the backwards-horse-riding got a big laugh and Dad looked like a spanner in his silly hat.

When the lights came up, all the pupils and teachers were standing at the front of the hall. Together.

"Most irregular," said Mr Dewdrop.

"No, I'll allow it," said the mayor, who was acting like a judge in a big trial on TV. "I want to see where they're going with this."

Mr Keane walked forward. "Geography isn't about rocks and weather fronts and – heaven help us – longshore flipping drift," he said. "Geography is about people and how they live. It's about nature and our world. And it teaches us about not making things worse and how to make things better, that's all. And I'm really sorry if I forgot that somewhere along the way."

Dr Nobel put a kindly hand on his shoulder. "Today, too many neighbours are fighting, because they can't share land and they can't share resources."

"It seemed to us that they're giving geography a bad name," said Miss Hunny.

"That, and the fact that a lot of geography at school is dead boring," said Rufus.

"So we decided that the schools shouldn't fight either," said Misses Eyre and Austen.

"And we thought the very best way to celebrate our planet…" said Plum.

"Was to say 'bum' to the stupid competition," said Penny.

"And to present today a JOINT project," said Mr Rainbow.

The men from the Nice 'N' Neat Countryside Alliance looked unhappy.

But the audience from the town clapped and cheered.

When it was silent again, Nat reached into a box and took out what looked like a tiny rock.

"With both schools working together, this is what we achieved," she said. "This is the head of what we believe to be a brand-new dinosaur, found this week, right here in the cliffs of Lower Snot— er, Totley. It'll be sent to the Natural History Museum to be checked. It could be a major find."

There was applause.

"But who ACTUALLY found it?" said Mr Dewdrop. "WHO?"

Everyone ignored him.

"It doesn't matter," said Dr Nobel, "it was a team effort."

"This morning we're talking about living together and SHARING," said Mr Keane.

"And working WITH each other," said Sky.

"And looking after the world," said Professor Paradise, jumping up and joining in. "Yes! Get in! YOU TELL 'EM!"

"And having some FUN!" shouted Mr Keane. "This is a fun world. Anyone remember FUN around here?"

The audience cheered and clapped.

"I think you may have forgotten," said Sky over the sounds of drumming, coming from outside and getting closer. "Let's go outside. I want to show you all something."

She led everyone outside, to where an amazing sight was marching up the high street towards them.

After five long years, the carnival was back in Lower Totley.

"With our lovely lady mayor's permission, we organised this carnival," said Sky. "You see, we might have forgotten fun, but our neighbouring towns haven't. And they've brought some people along to help us remember! So, let's welcome:

"The Giants from Upper Totley!

"The Mad Morris Maniacs of Melton Swingely!

"The Carnival Queen OAP Belly Dance Troupe from Longham Market!

"The Barmy Bongo Drums of Bolton-on-Hassock!

"The Twirly Majorettes from Spong!

"And the Fire-breathers from Much-Farting-on-the-Marsh!"

The carnival procession, with all its music and streamers and bunting and costumes, swept by, picking up volume and townspeople as it went.

"YOU'RE RUINING EVERYTHING," yelled Mr Dewdrop, hopping about with the other grey people from the Nice 'N' Neat Countryside Alliance. "You're just going to make a mess."

He was bonked on the head by an Upper Totley giant.

"Mr Bungee, stop them," Mr Dewdrop yelled,

"or we won't book your camp for our competition again."

But when Nat turned to look, it was as if Mr Bungee had gone mad.

"I don't care," he yelled. "We're closing the camp. We don't like you. We don't even like kids."

"Then why've you been a kids' camp leader?" asked Dr Nobel, who looked angry.

"How many jobs do you know where you can walk around all day playing in the mud and making camp?" said Mr Bungee, swaying in the breeze. "But now we've discovered gold on our site. Gold, I say! So all you kids and you teachers, you can all... get lost."

He held out a chunk of rock. Bits of it glittered.

Nat looked at Darius. "I recognise that," she said.

Darius looked blank.

Mr Bungee skipped with joy. "We blew up half the hillside yesterday when we discovered it, and there's tons of the stuff. HA!"

"It's true," said Mrs Ferret. "We're turning the eco camp into the largest open-face gold mine in the country."

"That's not very eco," said Dad, dodging a drum majorette.

"I'm fed up of eco, you big Green Bogey," shouted Mrs Ferret, whose voice was slurry. "I'm fed up of everything being made of wood and string, and food tasting of soil, and having to dig our own loos! I'm going to build a big tower block made of gold and I'll live at the very top, looking down on the rest of you."

Then she started dancing with Mr Bungee.

Nat watched the performance open-mouthed.

Darius and Sky, standing next to her, looked less surprised for some reason.

"Do you know," said Professor Paradise, coming up to them, "why scientists think the zombie-frog is called the zombie-frog?"

"Course I don't," said Nat. "I got twelve per cent in my last biology test." Then she looked at Mr Bungee again and thought a bit harder. "Hmm," she said.

Professor Paradise smiled a slow smile. "It's because the juice from a squeezed frog is extremely alcoholic. One drop of it in, say, a glass of delicious orange juice, will make the drinker extremely drunk – and make them act like a zombie."

"Oh, interesting," said Nat.

"It's VERY interesting," said Professor Paradise, watching Mr Bungee and Mrs Ferret do the conga.

Darius shrugged.

Sky shrugged.

The reclusive eco professor looked between them. "I'm not going to ask any more questions," he said, "but it would be very nice if Cedric was returned to his tank today and he wasn't squeezed any more."

He wandered off to join in a spot of morris dancing.

"Darius," said Nat, "what was actually in your evil orange juice of sneaky doom?"

Darius looked at her. "Do you want me to answer that question?" he said.

"What question?" said Nat.

"I've got a tiny question too," said Penny. "Was it a massive coincidence that someone told Mr Bungee there was gold on his land *on the very same day* we needed tons of rock shifted so we could find a new fossil?"

"Ooh, I hadn't thought of that," said Nat. "Nice one, Penny. You're not just a pretty face."

Penny smiled and gave her friend a hug.

Then they both grabbed Darius, who looked alarmed.

"If we squeezed *you* really hard," laughed Nat, "what would we get?"

"I'm not risking it," said Penny, letting go.

"Why is it," said Mum, as they watched the noisy, messy, *fun* carnival parade trundle down the high street, "that anything and everything your dad touches ends in some kind of total chaos?"

"Because he's the Green Bogey," laughed Sky. "Hadn't you heard?"

"Very true," said Dad.

"Sorry I've ruined your new career," said Nat. "I think you'll be getting a terrible report."

"I think Mr Dewdrop should be more worried about his silly organisation's future," laughed Sky.

"Besides, the world's a better place without your father working with criminals," said Mum. "Darius is bad enough."

"Thanks," said Darius, from somewhere.

"He has got a job today though," said Sky. "I wasn't kidding about the Green Bogey – it's just what the carnival needs. And the mayor wants *you*. Do well, and she'll write you all the Approved for Kids certificates you need."

"What do I do?"

"Lead the parade," said Sky.

"Winner," said Dad.

Nat cringed. She had thought the week was over. But no.

"Remind everyone," said Mr Keane, "what happens to the Green Bogey at the end?"

"Oh, he's killed to release his spirit back into the wild," said Sky. "It's a very old tradition."

"Right," said Dad. "Now, I'm not being ungrateful or anything, but I do have a prior engagement."

"They don't kill YOU, silly," laughed Sky. "They just light a bonfire and chuck something of yours in."

"Your mother?" said Mum. She looked around. "Joking, obviously."

"Something like… my green hat?" said Dad, frowning at Mum.

"Exactly like your hat," said Sky.

"Finally!" said Nat. "Can I chuck in your rotten ukulele too?"

The End

Don't miss the rest of Nathalia Buttface's cringe-tastic adventures...